TRAPPED!

Chris stopped in his tracks, hearing a noise behind him, and knew even before he turned around that it was a bear! The morose and terrifying animal was back near the rock ledge, walking erect and coming toward him with its head down.

That posture signaled its intention to fight, and the boy wasted no time in scrambling out to open ground. He ran up the slope and heard, when he reached the top, the bear's tremendous bulk crashing through the undergrowth.

Knowing he had to be quick, Chris sprinted toward the nearest tree. For all its fat, the bear could still run as fast as a dog. . . .

WHITE WATER, STILL WATER
was originally published by
Doubleday & Company, Inc.

Critics' Corner:

"The fear and panic that the young can feel in the face of disaster, as well as the courage, fortitude, and will to live they somehow can summon forth, are pointed up with force and clarity . . . an absorbing tale by an author who obviously understands boys and the out-of-doors."

—*The Chicago Tribune*

"The reactions of an easygoing daydreamer when faced with solving the harsh practical problems of survival in the woods are realistically portrayed in an unusual adventure story."

—*A.L.A. Booklist*

"The story of his shipwreck, wandering for a hundred days through all kinds of weather, his fight for food and primitive shelter until his dog and family find him again is truly a boy's adventure with poetic overtones that any boy of spirit will follow with fascination."

—*San Francisco Chronicle & Examiner*

Other Recommendations: Bulletin of the Center for Children's Books, University of Chicago; Child Study Association; Bro-Dart Foundation, Elementary School Library Collection; Library Journal (especially recommended).

About the Author and the Illustrator:

J. ALLAN BOSWORTH began writing while still a radioman aboard the USS *Missouri*. World War II had just ended, and the ship was on her long voyage home. A native Californian, he returned to San Francisco and took a job at the *Chronicle*. Ten years later, having published two novels and a few dozen short stories, he left the newspaper to begin writing on a full-time basis. He and his wife and two daughters now live in Salem, Virginia. *All the Dark Places* is another of his books for young readers.

CHARLES W. WALKER received his art training at Syracuse University, College of Fine Arts. He has illustrated many books for children and is currently an illustrator for a large advertising agency in New York City.

WHITE WATER, STILL WATER

by J. Allan Bosworth

Illustrated by Charles W. Walker

AN ARCHWAY PAPERBACK
WASHINGTON SQUARE PRESS • NEW YORK

WHITE WATER, STILL WATER

An Archway Paperback edition

1st printing.........................April, 1969
2nd printing.......................August, 1970

L

Published by Washington Square Press,
a division of Simon & Schuster, Inc., 630 Fifth Avenue, New York, N.Y.

WASHINGTON SQUARE PRESS editions are distributed in the
U.S. by Simon & Schuster, Inc., 630 Fifth Avenue, New
York, N.Y. 10020 and in Canada by Simon & Schuster
of Canada, Ltd., Richmond Hill, Ontario, Canada.

Standard Book Number: 671-29320-6.
Library of Congress Catalog Card Number: 66-11729.

Chapter One

The river began somewhere in Canada. It grew, coming south, turning wider and deeper and more certain in its run for the sea. Where it passed the Holm cabin, its voice had become big enough to send a cool whispering far into the forest, to the mountains on either side.

Only in the unsettling and violent spring, when the snow retreated, did the water become angry. And then, the ground and the very air shook with it. There in the loft under the steep pitch of the roof, where young Christian Holm always slept, it could almost seem as if the valley were drowning and the once solid earth might crumble away.

It was not something that had ever frightened him. He had been born in the cabin, and the river was no less a part of his life than the sun and stars

1

or this brilliance of autumn that, harmless fire, now burned in the forest.

But he liked most the way the river ran in summer, and the way it was now. The part he knew flowed, peaceful and singing, past a crescent shore of rounded stones. Swift trout ran the bright water, hunting the blue-sparking dragonflies. And toward the center, the dark currents were hurried, dark as the trees beyond, and like the trees, remembering the spring that was, and the spring that would come again.

He walked a few feet along the crescent. The stones came down and were left by the river in the spring, and myriad small frogs lived among them during low water. They swarmed, leaping in at his approach.

Sometimes, Christian brought a jar and scrambled across the stones until, wet and breathless, he caught a dozen or so. They were quick and elusive and, because of that, something to be prized. But, too, they were part of the river; this lovely mystery that forever sought the sea. He never kept the pop-eyed creatures for long.

Chris went on to where the stones ended and then stepped back onto the soft and quieter earth. Just beyond him, the tall pines again marched down to meet the water, and he stopped to look back at the clearing.

Griper, the big black Labrador, was coming at a lumbering trot to join him. But his father was still out in the forest with the wagon, cutting and loading the last of the firewood for the long winter soon coming. His mother, Louisa, was in the cabin taking a little nap before starting supper. Neither of them would see him walk into the trees; where he was going and what he did there was a secret he had kept all summer long and, now, most of the autumn.

He knew it was wrong to go sneaking off like that. Chris wanted to tell them about the raft he had made. There was no one else with whom he could share it. The nearest people were at the settlement thirty miles upriver, and he did not know anyone his own age. They made the trip only once a month.

But his mother would put a stop to it if she knew. She would point out that he was a poor swimmer, and care not at all that the shallows were quiet and, at worst, reached only to his chin. It seemed part of that little, dark-haired woman's nature always to be there, soft-voiced, with wide apron standing between him and anything she could not completely trust. The nearest doctor, she emphasized, was in the settlement; he was both physician and veterinarian, and one could never be sure his methods were not intended for horses.

As for his father, well, if Eric Holm ever found out, the raft would probably wind up on the wood-pile for an entirely different reason.

His father was upset enough as it was over the time he spent reading the few books they owned and those he borrowed from the man who ran the general store at Bodwin's Landing, the way he neglected his chores, and especially the hours he spent "mooning" down by the river. How would dreaming on a raft be any different?

A boy living on a hundred-and-sixty-acre homestead in the middle of a wilderness, a *real* boy, would be out hunting and exploring and running a trapline. In the winter, a boy would learn to use the big skis that had been made for him, and not stay by the fire so much, wishing winter were gone.

Chris tugged at Griper's ears and then slipped into the forest, hurrying across the shadowed quarter-mile or so to where the raft waited.

A *real* boy . . . yes, it had come to that. Only a few nights ago, when he was in the loft and supposedly asleep, he had heard them talking. Chris remembered everything that was said.

"You lose your temper with him too often, Eric."

And Eric Holm, with his Norwegian accent, had replied, "Maybe. Guess I'm not a patient man. But he's not like other boys. There's no spirit to him, no hardness to his bones. The games he plays are so quiet, and I can't get much work out of him. I don't even think he even likes it here!"

"Chris is only thirteen," Louisa reminded the slim, blond giant. "Still a child."

"Child? At thirteen I was already a year with the fishing fleet at Larvik! You hold him too close, Louisa."

She ignored the reference to herself, saying, "And doing it much too soon."

Eric sighed. "Maybe. But I'll tell you something. Even when I wasn't working, I played hard and looked for adventure. I didn't daydream or lie around all day reading books!"

"It's good to read."

"Sure! I know. I'm glad he can read, and do arithmetic. He writes better than me. You're a good teacher, Louisa. You had to be," he chuckled, "to teach me English. But there's a time to put books away! And it's time he stopped playing with his little soldiers I carved. And drawing foolish pictures of places he's never seen! He ought to run more, climb trees, and spend time with a good axe in his hands. I want him to be strong and useful! What if I break my leg tomorrow?"

"We'd get by," Louisa said, and it was typical of her. Although she was small, utterly feminine, and not really at ease in the wilderness, she could also be quite stubborn.

"Would we?" he snorted at her remark. "This is no place for half a man to depend on half a boy!"

"Eric!"

"Maybe I say the wrong things. He's our son, and I love him. But it's still true. He *isn't* like other boys. You got to turn loose a little, Louisa. Let him grow!"

Unhappily, he guessed his father was right and,

for a long time after, he had waited in the dark for sleep to cover sadness.

He *did* like it there. It was home. Maybe someday he would plant his feet in the furrows and feel as his father did—this man with the North Sea eyes who found such joy in grasping that earth between river and mountain and making a world of his own spring from it. But, for now, there was a bigger and more exciting world beyond. And if it kept him from being all that a father hoped and expected of a boy, he could not help it. That other world was full of people and uncounted wonders, and he longed to see them.

Chris stopped, both startled and delighted by a bull elk that suddenly bounded away. He grabbed the dog to put an end to the barking, and waited, listening as the sound of running turned soft in the forest and was lost. They went on, then, with the dank smell of the marsh growing in the air.

Just ahead, where the trees opened to the sky again, the edge of the river slipped into a shallow basin and, barely seeming to move, found its way back into the channel. But some of the water seeped across low ground to form the marsh that stretched eastward almost to the foot of the mountain.

The marsh was quiet, now; it was too late in the year. Snow might come at any time. The danger was foretold by the dry rattle of gusting leaves, and in the quiet, brittle air when the sun was down. And so they were gone; the ducks that lived here

and rose in throbbing clouds when he came, and the nobler geese.

No more than a week ago he heard them passing—the big Canadians touching the cold moon and winging south to leave the nights behind haunted with their cries.

How alike they were! The geese and the river, and the spell they could cast, whispering of things beyond the mountains, the downwind places he had never seen.

Chris and the dog reached the water then, that blurred division between river and marsh where reeds begin to thicken. The raft was almost hidden in them, close to the bank. Holding on to a tree root, he reached out and pulled it free.

It was not a big raft, being about four feet wide and perhaps twice that in length. The pine logs were tied together with bits of rope and wire, and had two crosspieces for stiffening. Standing at the back was a forked limb to hold the sweep, and the latter was only a slender pole with a short piece of board nailed to the end; awkward and not of much use. But then, the raft was not meant to go anywhere. The miles it traveled, the distant shores it found, were only dreamed.

"You stay here, Griper."

Chris gingerly crawled onto the center of the logs and, with a kick of his foot, pushed away from the bank. The raft drifted for a moment on the quiet water of the shallows, and then rested there as gently as a fallen leaf between marsh and river. Looking back at the patiently waiting Labrador, and smiling a little, the boy stretched out on his back and closed his eyes.

He did not have very much time. It was only around three when he left the cabin, and there were still a couple of hours left before the chill of evening would come creeping across the shallows. Even so, his mother would want the wood-box filled before she started supper; he had let it get too low again. But, he sighed, it did not really matter. The river, without coming to him or he to it, nevertheless touched him here. With voice and faint stirrings beneath the raft, it gave him within the space of a breath the gift of a thousand miles.

In the dark behind his lids, and dreaming, he rushed away for that world beyond forest and mountains, hurried to find towns and cities, other people, and to see that place where the river finally lost itself in the Pacific.

He knew it by heart, and yet relished every changing mile. The cabin was already far behind, forgotten. Time no longer existed, and even now he could see the first glittering towers rising in the distance.

Something new touched the raft and made it tremble. Chris opened his eyes wide with sudden alarm and saw the pale sky above him slanting and quickly beginning to turn. The tops of trees clustered around the edges of his vision were dipping down at a sickening angle, and then rising swiftly to lean the other way.

He rolled over quickly to look, and knew at once what had happened. Sensing the boy's fear, even Griper saw the danger and had jumped to his feet to whine and bark. Caught on some quiet and unexpected eddying in the shallows, the raft had drifted across the inlet to reach the river itself!

Chris got to his knees and made a frantic grab for the sweep. As fast as he could, he worked it from side to side, trying to force the raft back from the river's grasp. But it was already too late; the current had him now and would not turn loose.

As the raft pitched and gathered speed, the banks rushed past, and that short stretch of river familiar to him fell swiftly behind. Griper was trying to follow along the bank. He caught quick glimpses of the dog charging through heavy brush and between the trees. Twice, the big retriever even came bounding into the edges of the water with the obvious intention of challenging the currents. But each time he thought better of it and fell a little farther behind.

There was no hope in it. For all his strength and simple devotion to a young master, Griper was powerless to help. And what lay ahead could only be guessed. Just one chance remained, and the boy seized upon it desperately. Try to steer, he told himself. Try to steer toward the bank, and then jump off while there is time!

Chris pushed on the slender pole with all his

10

might. It bent, trembling in his grip, but nothing happened. In that moment of terror, he thought of the cabin back in the quiet clearing, and cried out for his mother. Panic-stricken and not daring to swim from there, he sobbed and plunged the sweep deeper into the water to get more leverage. It had to work! It just had to, or else what was he to do?

For a brief moment, the raft began to turn and swing closer to the shore. And for that moment he knew a little hope. But then the sweep found bottom and, colliding with a submerged boulder, tore itself from his hands and struck him on the side of his head.

A stabbing pain, darkness; there was nothing more.

Chapter Two

For a moment Chris did not know where he was or what had happened. It was beyond understanding, to open his eyes and discover darkness thundering about him, and in that darkness, to see one glittering star gone mad. Wild and brilliant, it struck deep to the far edge of the universe and then careened back again. Chris groaned at the sight and turned away.

He knew he was on the raft, and that was as it should be; he remembered, now, walking to where it was hidden and climbing on for his imagined journey. But this icy blackness . . . it should have been late afternoon, with blue-smoke sky and those curious columns of gnats rising in the last of the warmth, or the even softer hour beyond that, when marsh frogs began to speak, and the first small bat came to search the quiet chill of mountain shadows.

The raft plunged abruptly and began to spin. Water exploded against log-ends and, so cold it felt like liquid fire, drenched him thoroughly. Chris rolled over on his stomach and, sickened by the realization of where he was, raised up on his elbows to look. But pain shot through his head and made him fall back again.

The river was all around him, rolling and dimly glistening. Caught on the backbone of the current, the raft was as helpless as a fallen leaf. The boy pressed his face hard against familiar logs and cried out. For an instant the frail note hung in the air and then, fading, blew away.

Chris felt himself slowly slipping back; the dark in his mind that was deeper than the night reached up to claim him again and he fought against it. What little strength remained sparked and protested within, telling him to get off the raft. He had been on it since before sundown, and how long ago was that? Only God knew how far he had come. *Now,* he told himself. Try to swim before you are carried any farther!

But the cold and the hurting pressed down on him and he could barely move his arms; the dark thing crept closer. *Rest,* it whispered. *Rest. It isn't time.*

How long he went on that way, caught and floating in the dimly defined space between oblivion and awareness, Chris could not know. There were intervals of deep peace, where nothing existed, and times when he came a little higher to that place where dreams abound.

Home and the clearing, the dog Griper, and Bodwin's Landing, Eric and Louisa Holm . . . they came in fragments and without sensible order, and after a while Chris knew even in the middle of them that they were illusions and no more real than the glorious phantom bears Griper sometimes chased, as he slept by the fireside. Still, they were islands of safety and warmth and the boy grasped at them desperately, trying to find the one that would last and, like his mother's arms, hold him away from the truth.

But then the terrible cold would come flooding in to destroy it, and he would find himself clinging to the raft, rushing farther and farther from home.

It was from the Landing's general store that he came this time, and almost certain that the taste of picklebrine was still on his lips, awakened to a new and greater thundering.

The raft plunged and twisted, pitched brutally beneath him. Chris, starting to roll off, grabbed frantically for a new grip on the cross-piece and held on. The water here was white with fury, and he sensed rather than saw black and glistening walls of rock closing in.

Shocked into it, his mind was suddenly clear.

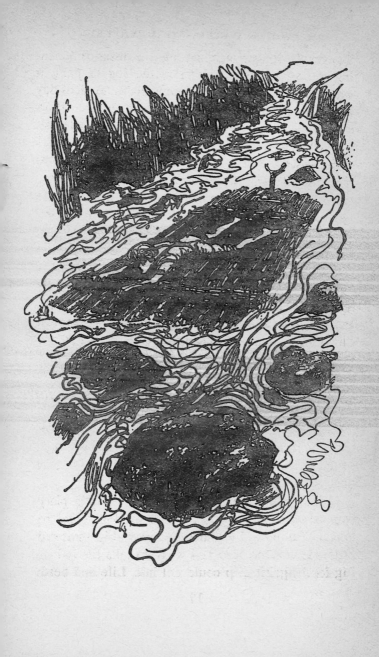

if he didn't stop to eat and rest. Life and death

20

Danger no longer waited behind a dozen threatening guises so easily hidden in the fog of pain; it was sharply defined and immediate. A half-day upstream from the clearing, there was a short stretch of river where the same thing happened. Chris had seen it many times from the wagon.

So violent that spray rose high into the air to hang like steam, water exploded through narrow canyons and shot down rock-strewn raceways to boil in the caldrons of sudden turns. More storm than river, it fought viciously to escape and, at last, foamed into a darkly peaceful pool at the other end. . . .

Without warning, the raft dipped murderously and was thrust upward to ride nearly on edge. Before Chris knew what had happened, it slammed down again to leave him halfway in the water and barely hanging on with one hand.

The current sucked at him and tried to drag him in; it was an almost impossible task to get one leg up, and then the other. But he had managed no more than that when the logs jarred across submerged rock and sent him slipping back. It happened twice before the boy finally inched his way back to the center.

Moments ago Chris had wondered if this place was as short as the one upriver, or if it might be longer. But now he realized it probably mattered little. He was too cold and weak to take the battering for long; his grip could not last. Life and death came close together in his numbed and straining fingers.

Half-drowned, barely able to gasp for breath, he could only live one minute at a time and hope the raft would not overturn or shatter on some waiting boulder before the next minute could begin. There was not even time to find the words his mother had given him and pray.

On and on it went, not letting up for an instant. Turning and twisting, bursting through one tortured labyrinth after another, the river persisted in the nightmare it had created. If there was silence beyond this booming place, he could not hear it. If there was quiet water near at hand, Chris could not sense any promise of it in chaos.

But something else had been slowly creeping into his awareness. It was not recognizable at first; like some shy echo, it was too often drowned out in the storming. And now, with the horror of it striking deep, he knew what it was.

Never intended for what they had to withstand here, the bindings of wire and old rope were gradually giving way. He could feel the logs spreading and closing beneath him. Even the crosspiece had become loose in his hands.

Chris closed his eyes, feeling something wither inside. He did not know by what right he had managed to hang on this long. He should have been dead; common sense would have predicted it. And yet, hang on he had, and he wanted to go on trying for as long as hands and arms would let him. But now, what was the use?

If once there had been any hope at all, it was gone now. Nothing could be done to stop it from happening. The logs would keep working at the bindings until finally they parted. Indeed, it could come even more quickly. The next time the raft straddled and grated across a boulder might be enough to do it. And then?

He could not survive by clinging to one slender log. Not here.

All foam and spray, the water rioted through a bend and then gathered itself to rush downward straight and swift. Chris felt one log go, when the raft crashed against the wall in that bend, and another as it scudded and dipped into the race. The time had come, then . . .

With paralyzing speed the raft hurtled toward a dim whiteness far below. Chris could not breathe. Wind pressed against his face and tore at his lips, and for a moment he remembered a day when he was very small, remembered clasping arms and legs around his father's back and shrieking with joy as they whipped down a slope. With the great Norwegian skis hissing in the snow, there had been a wind such as this.

The world was made of silver, when he found it again, and morning was at hand. A brilliant moon had risen from the gray rim of dawn, and where there had been only blackness there were now trees and sleeping mountains. Of all that Chris had known in the night, only the sharp and brittle cold remained. The cold, and a distant thundering.

Morning. . . . Chris sucked air into his lungs and rolled over on his side, not yet ready to believe he could still be alive. For a minute or so, he might even have slept again, but then the cold persisted and the meaningless sound in the distance nagged.

Stiff and sore, and feeling as if every muscle were weighted with lead, he came up on one arm to blink at the river. It was wide here and, not seeming to move, peacefully mirrored the moon.

Chris wanted to lie down again and forget it, forget everything for a while. But then he saw the raft, what was left of it, barely hanging together. The river would not go on this way forever. That roaring . . .

The boy slowly got to his knees and, looking for the sweep, was not surprised to see that both it and the fork that held it had been carried away. But he had to get off now, before time ran out. There was only one way.

Reluctantly and, in his exhaustion, terribly uncertain, Chris lowered himself into the water. He hung on to the doubtful security of the raft for a moment longer, and then struck out for the shore.

It was perhaps forty feet away; so close and yet so very deceptive. The current, slow and ponderous, grasped and carried him downstream faster than he could move forward. He knew then that he might yet die . . . come to an end not in white water as he had expected so many times, but ironically in a lovely mirror where trees and sky, as in a quiet dream, could be found again. And the prospect no longer frightened him.

There simply was no space in those last agonizing minutes for anything but the struggle to which he had become irrevocably committed. Minutes? It felt much longer than that. Blinded by his own splashing and barely able to stay afloat, he might as well have been a grain of sand or a piece of drifting wood. For all his efforts the river still did with him as it pleased.

It was, then, only by accident and out of the whim of a wandering current that he finally felt the bottom come up to scrape his legs.

Gratefully Chris stood up and stumbled the rest of the way to reach dry sand. He swayed for a moment, waiting for Griper to come and greet him. Dazedly he dropped to his knees. Dawn . . . it was *yesterday* he had last seen his companion! Griper was not here. He would be home now. Yes, at home . . .

Seeing a clump of willow growing in a sheltered hollow between two massive boulders, the boy crawled to it and, there, surrendered to sleep once more.

Chapter Three

The sun was late in coming, that time of year, and was later still in reaching the deep, wandering canyons of the river. Even when it touched and warmed the ridges, high beyond the march of timber, the night's last owl could yet be found skimming silently homeward in the dark forest below.

Not until the golden light slipped down the mountains to the west and crept, pale and broken, across the canyon floor to river's edge, did night truly end.

Christian Holm had not moved. Lying face downward in the sand between the boulders, and locked in deep, dreamless sleep, he was oblivious to morning's arrival. Rigid with cold and hardly seeming alive, the boy did not stir or visibly begin to breathe until the stone walls of his sanctuary caught and held the heat of the sun.

It was a long journey, from the pit of sleep to that first, dim awakening. In the dark behind his lids, Chris knew only that he was warm. Then, a vague fear passed through him when he remembered where he was. But reality was pushed aside; being warm was too wonderful. Chris did not want to know anything beyond this heavenly state, and so nothing else existed.

As the sun climbed higher, the gentle wrapping began to dissolve. Even though the boy fought against it by trying to move back into unknowing sleep, it had to be. Just as there is a moment when the last drop of dew starts returning to the air, and the blade of grass that held it straightens toward the morning, there had to be a time when the world reached in to find him.

It began with hunger. Chris had not eaten in nearly twenty-four hours. Too, having slept his fatigue away, it was impossible to shut out the sudden and raucous cry of birds, or not to feel gnats tickling across his face. And the river . . . he could hear it rumbling somewhere downstream. But, most of all, it had become too hot where he was. The space between the boulders, once pleasantly warm, had turned into an oven.

Damp with sweat and gasping for breath, Chris crawled out into the open and, standing up, went to the river's edge.

Kneeling over the bright, clear water, he

scooped it up and drank until thirst was gone, and then splashed it across his face and hair. The boy held still, looking down to watch the water dripping from his hair to make quick rings on the surface.

For a minute or two, he listened to his father's axe biting into wood, and the lordly crowing of the Cornish rooster. Griper's deep voice resounded in the clearing. And his mother was singing as she wielded her broom. But the sounds were only in his mind. They were no more than inventions, illusions as fragile as the rings of water and just as quickly gone.

He was not by the clearing. The cabin would not be there if he turned around. Chris knew it, but he had not gone beyond the mere fact. Watching this quietly shifting surface, he still would not look at or accept what his eyes and brain told him were there. In the mirror he saw the wavering reflections of a strange sky and unfamiliar trees and nothing more.

Only when he got up to leave was Chris aware for an instant of the other image . . . a face beneath a wet tangle of blond hair, with a swollen upper lip and a darkly bruised cheekbone. And the eyes, gray and questioning . . .

The boy turned away, feeling terror. But it was a brief and fleeting thing, like the shadow of a crow passing across the ground.

He had no way of telling how long he was actually on the raft, or how many times it might have caught on a snag or a rock to hang for a while, or only drifted lazily as it had been doing when he abandoned it and swam ashore.

Nevertheless, Chris admitted, the river had probably carried him several miles. The thing to do now was to find out where he was and then start heading back without any more delay. The day was half gone already, and he wanted to get home before the sun went down and the air turned cold again.

He was barefooted, and wore only a thin, short-sleeved shirt and a pair of old pants that were cut off at the knees. His clothes were dry now, but in that high autumn air night would still be an ordeal.

A mile or so to the east of the cabin and the clearing were two mountains lying parallel to the river. One did not have any particular features to set it apart from the rest of the range. But the other, to the south of it, was saddle-shaped. Its horn rose above timberline, a shamble of gray, windblown rock where only a few stunted and gnarled little pines managed to cling.

All he had to do, Chris reasoned, was climb until he reached a place where there were no trees to block the view. Then, seeing the saddle, he would know how far he had to go and the exact direction.

It would be foolish, he told himself, not to check the direction and the lay of the land. The river did not cut a straight line across the wilderness as it rolled away toward the southwest. It went, curving and bending, like a giant and shining serpent.

And what if, for a while, it had fallen more to the west to make a long and gentle turn before coming past this place? A lot of time might be saved by cutting across country to meet the river farther on.

Chris put the sandy shore behind him and began the climb up through the forest. He wished he had his boots, but there was no point in worrying about that now. Besides, there under the trees the ground was carpeted with a thick layer of pine needles that were soft and cool beneath his feet.

He thought of home as he went, and how good it would be to get back. The boy had never been away from home before, except to go to Bodwin's Landing once a month with a load of vegetables, and maybe a bundle of newly cured furs for trading. But then it was always with his mother and father, the three of them perched on the narrow seat.

Home . . . his mother would be beside herself with worry, and Eric would be searching everywhere for him. When he got back, they would make a big fuss and then start asking questions. If he admitted to having built a raft, they would both be angry. Time and time again his mother had warned him about the river. And what his father would have to say about foolish daydreaming was not pleasant to contemplate.

Chris stopped to get his breath, wondering if

there was something else he could tell them. What else could have happened?

For some reason he remembered his favorite book, the one called *Kidnapped*. He did not suppose Eric Holm would believe it for a minute if he said he had been carried off by a mysterious trapper, or a band of hunters . . . no, probably not.

The boy thought about telling them that he had just wandered off and could not find his way back. But even that would be hard to swallow when all he had to do was listen for the river, get back to it, and follow it to the clearing.

Chris saw unbroken sunlight ahead. A moment later he stepped into a narrow clearing that climbed the mountainside to a rocky bluff before the trees closed in again.

As he went around the side and up to stand on the shelf of rock, his attention was drawn again to the thundering that came from somewhere downstream. The sound was louder here; he was far above the forest that had muffled it before. Looking down, he searched for its source.

The river went past the spot where he had spent the night, rolled through a heavily wooded turn and began to pick up speed. Turning white, it shot into a cloud of spray, and disappeared! Only by taking a few steps to the right was he able to see it again—a short stretch of foaming water running sixty or seventy feet lower than where it vanished.

"Falls!" Chris sucked in his breath. If he had stayed on the raft just a few minutes more . . .

It was not so much the idea of dying, even though the plunge most certainly would have been fatal. He was awed by it, but the last moment of his life had approached unnoticed and then retreated to belong once more to some other time. The thought he found so dismaying now was that of being caught in that white water and being swept helplessly to the very edge of nothing, and falling . . . falling.

It prickled at the backs of his knees and in the soles of his feet, and almost made him sit down. Chris looked away, took a deep breath, and moved across the bluff until trees stood between him and the sight of it.

Returning with some relief to the purpose of his climb, Chris followed the course of the river until it was lost from sight, and looked all along the northern horizon.

They were not there. The boy could not even see the mountains of home.

Chapter Four

Emptiness and all the vast, shrieking silences crowded in on him and drowned out even the tempest where water fell. Stunned and shaken, Chris desperately searched the ragged horizon in the vain hope that he would yet discover what he wanted to see.

Mountains did not vanish! They did not shatter and crumble or in a night give way to the winds that raged at them. The familiar saddle had to be there somewhere with its southern summit, if nothing else, shouldering above its neighbors.

He studied the path of the sun and reaffirmed that part of the horizon he had identified as being north. Knowing the river had carried him generally toward the southwest, he had only to turn his eyes a little to the right. Yes, the saddle's horn would reach higher than any mountain he could see. But northeast, northwest or anywhere between, it was not in sight. And all the conjuration in the world would not make it rise to beckon and reassure.

Woodenly, Chris came down off the bluff and half-walked, half-trotted back toward the river. Glancing over his shoulder once at the open space before leaving it, he told himself that it was a simple matter of not having climbed far enough.

A little mountain could hide a larger one in the distance behind it. Surely, if he walked for a while and then climbed to a high place again, the saddle would be there, big and comforting.

He just was not that far from home. It was unreasonable to expect anyone to lie unconscious on a flimsy little raft and be carried for long or very far.

The river had awakened him when it turned rough and went faster, had it not? Of course! He remembered that happening, and even then, the raft could not have gone any great distance; it had only seemed that way because it was dark and he was frightened. In all probability, most of the night had been spent sleeping on slow, quiet water. How could it be any other way?

The boy reached the river again and, thirsty from his climb, stopped at its edge to drink. The rings in the water, his face and eyes looking back . . . the trees and sky that did not belong to memory . . . he saw these things once more and suddenly began to sob.

None of it was true!

Like someone afraid of the dark, he had pulled the blanket of self-deception over his head and closed his eyes to all the demons there. And they had not gone away.

The truth was that his flimsy little raft *had* endured, he *had* clung to it beyond all reasonable expectations, and the proof was in the mountains he had observed from the bluff. Only seeming to be close in that clear autumn air, those on the horizon were probably as much as forty miles away and maybe more. Home and its mountains were beyond them, somewhere, but how far beyond was a frightening question still to be answered.

Only one thing was certain. He had been carried deep into a vast, uninhabited region that stretched south from his father's homestead for some two or three hundred empty miles.

To be so very far from home, and then add to grim measure the fact that he had kept the raft a secret . . . his mind balked at the enormity of it. Eric Holm would not know where to look for him! In ever widening and useless circles, his father would be combing the forest around the clearing.

Only Griper had seen what happened, and what could he do? The knowledge was locked forever within that broad, black skull. Restless and worrying, the dog *might* take to hanging around the shallows and, in so doing, attract attention to the spot. For a moment Chris saw a glimmer of hope in that possibility. But then, the shallows . . . what were they but a place where a boy might wade or chase frogs? His father certainly would not find anything there to make him suspect otherwise.

However Eric finally came to consider the river, it would not be in terms of a raft being swept away for mile after lonely mile.

And so he was by himself, without help, and hungry, and night was coming again. The sun, poised on the heights of early afternoon, even now crept inexorably downward. It would be dark and freezing and . . . with all of it gathering to shout in him at once, the boy turned reddened and anguished eyes to look upriver. A strangled sound fluttering in his throat, Chris scrambled free of the boulder-strewn shore and began to run.

He did not know how many times he blindly stumbled and fell and, gasping, got up to run again—as if hurrying could cancel time and miles and take him away somehow from frightening things.

He came to the pool of quiet water after running nearly a mile, winded and ready to drop. For one startled and grateful moment, Chris saw just the shallows and the soft border of reeds. So much, in that respect, did it resemble the inlet where he had kept the raft, the boy fell to his knees and came within a breath of calling out to his father.

It was only a trick of the mind. Frightened, and wanting badly to see familiar ground, he was far too ready to believe the slightest suggestion that he might have been wrong about everything.

But the illusion, like those fancied images seen in summer clouds, was gone with a second glance. A marsh did not extend eastward from this place, and the inlet was smaller; even the pattern of trees was different here.

Disappointed, but accepting it for what it was, Chris started to get up and, suddenly feeling faint, fell back. His whole body had begun to tremble with weakness; waves of heat surged through him like fever.

It did not come just from running, although he knew now how foolish that had been. He was hungry, so very hungry, and he lay down to moan with the bitterness of it.

He had to have something to eat. And what was there? A whole river of water waited to quench his thirst, and he could fill his stomach with it. But there was not any food, and Chris rolled over to stare at the treetops through distorting tears.

Yes, it was as simple and brutal as that.

It was less than an hour later that he moved, not from sleep, but from some torpid and unthinking place of mind. Chris only moved his head to look sideways across the water, as if to catch another breath and gather himself before getting up.

A bit of motion caught his eye . . . a tiny thing disturbing the stillness of that scene for the briefest part of time. A wink, a flickering; no more. It seemed to have happened atop what appeared to be, in dappled sun, a mound of stones and earth, and browning moss.

His stomach pinched and hurting, Chris looked beyond it and at the inviting water again, deciding it was time to drink his fill and go on. The sun was close to the western ridges now; not much light was left.

Dreading the coming darkness and even the lengthening shadows, he started to get up. But before he could do so, he saw the mound of stones and earth inexplicably move and change in shape to become a *cat,* an alert and tensely quivering bobcat.

Startled by the quick transformation, and holding his breath, Chris watched the brindled, tawny animal creep closer to the water in a muscled crouch. Its mouth yammered silently, and its eyes were fixed on one spot just a few feet from the edge.

The bobcat froze to become motionless for a minute longer. Then, with a long leap and a savage cry, it was in the water. Not long at its work, that fierce creature grabbed with its forepaws, thrust its head under to bite and kill, and emerged from the shallows dragging a large fish between its legs.

Chris, until now preoccupied with observing this sample of nature's violent ways, was made to remember his hunger by the sight of that fine, glistening fish.

How many times had he seen one like it sputter-

ing and popping in a pan on his mother's stove? It was beyond counting. He had never liked fish much, preferring chicken or pork and especially the elk meat Eric Holm's rifle often provided. But that did not matter now.

The fish represented food and a full stomach, and Chris wondered if there was not some way of getting it away from its owner.

Not knowing quite how to go about it, and forgetting how dangerous it could be to meddle with a bobcat, Chris jumped to his feet and ran toward it. The only thing he could think of was that maybe the animal, suddenly seeing him, would drop the fish and run.

Spotting him immediately, the bobcat displayed no such intention. It turned and crouched over its catch with flattened ears, growling and ready to fight.

Chris stopped with no more than twenty feet separating them. He brought his hands together with a loud clap and shouted, "Drop it! Get away from here!"

The bobcat only snarled more threateningly and stood its ground, and Chris realized then that he was seeing one more indication of how deep into the wilderness he had been carried.

Far from the thin scattering of civilization that clung in a rough and lonely circle to Bodwin's Landing, this creature had never before seen a human being. It had lived its life undisturbed and, therefore, had no reason to be afraid.

"You win," Chris whispered and began to back off. He had no desire to quarrel with a cat that weighed maybe thirty-five pounds and could fight with the awesome fury of devils.

The bobcat's yellow eyes, still blazing pools of anger, remained fastened on him until he was a more polite distance away. Chris waited while the animal seized the fish, looked in his direction once more, and walked off into the forest.

Feeling cheated and more starved than ever, Chris stretched out at the water's edge and drank until his stomach felt swollen. Even if the bobcat had abandoned it, Chris tried to console himself, what could he have done with the fish? There was no way of cooking it. He did not have a single match in his pocket, and it would not have mattered if he had a hundred after being as wet as he was last night.

Getting up, he walked around the rim of the inlet and followed the river again. He did not know what else to do.

The sun went down early, as it always did in the mountains. Far above, the sky remained bright for a long time after, and the river held some of it for remembering and became a blue ribbon winding through the shadowed forest.

Chris moved through the gathering chill until it was too dark to walk. He found a place by the river where boulders would ward off the night winds, if they came, and hold the heat of the day for a short while.

The boy sat there, frightened and lonely, wishing for a fire and something to eat. But there was nothing he could do except curl up against one of the boulders and try to sleep through what was coming.

Sleep . . . it did carry him away, though not to the hoped-for refuge. With designs of its own, it took the happy images of home he had wanted for dreams and thrust him into a dark and fitful delirium where phantom cats and bitter stars shrieked with cold.

Chapter Five

His father and mother were there in the dark. Chris heard their voices quite clearly. They were worried about him, not knowing where he was, and he got up to walk toward them. All he had to do was reach their side and everything would be all right. His mother would give him something to eat and see to it that he was warm. Find them . . . where? The voices were without direction and, no matter where he walked, never came any closer.

Chris, beginning to weep, frantically called out. But no answering cry came to save him. They were suddenly gone, and the river came rushing back into the silence where voices had been. The sound of the river, intense and burning cold, and the first thin light of dawn . . .

Through dim and uncertain eyes, Chris watched

the nebulous glowing and saw no meaning in it. He knew only the cold that gripped his bones with incredible and hurting fingers. The boy began to slip, to fall back into the waiting blackness. But there was something wrong about the way it reached for him, and he jerked his eyes open again.

Chris looked wildly around, frightened by that moment and wanting to escape it. He had to get up. Yes, something told him to get up and walk. If he did not . . .

Groaning, he searched the face of the boulder until his fingers found a grip, and then began inching his way up. He was not sure he could do it. Every muscle screamed and threatened to crack open from being cold for so long. But finally he was standing.

After several minutes of clinging helplessly to the boulder, Chris turned and let go. He took a first, tentative step, wobbled, and dared try a second. The way it felt, he might as well have been learning to walk all over again. Discouraged, the boy nearly wept until he saw once more that dim glow spreading across the sky. Further from numbing sleep, he knew what it was now and his heart quickened at the sight.

In the distance, beyond the mountains and a horizon or two away, the sun was rising; a day was turning warm. As if he could hasten its coming, Chris watched the stars disappear and went his staggering, halting way up the river's shore.

The boy was a mile or two upstream when the sun lifted above the ridge to the east. Away from the river's cluttered and inconsistent shore and keeping to the edge of the forest, he stumbled along in a slow, shuffling walk.

Another day had begun. But with home still impossibly far away, what could the hours hold except greater hunger, growing weakness and, with the horrors of night just ending, a bleak promise that the dark would inevitably come again. The knowledge blinded him to all else, and he walked as if caught in the mire of hopeless dreams.

Only the first, probing rays of the sun coming through the trees were strong enough to make him stop. He felt hints of its wonderful warmth and, seeing a solid, uninterrupted patch of gold on the sand below him, turned and went down to collapse in its miracle.

Chris huddled there, caught and luxuriating in the sun's spell. He was warm, and how nice it would be, he thought sleepily, to go on being warm and not think about anything . . . to be like a stone or a flower, or no more than a bit of wood half-buried in that comforting sand.

"No!" Chris nearly shouted and stood up, his voice small and strange in that emptiness. The flower in his pleasant picturing had gone, and the bit of wood was not wood at all but gleaming bone . . . a *rib* . . . jutting from the sand!

Close to panic again, and hurrying, the boy picked his way around the rocks to the river's edge. Warm for the first time in ages, he did not like the idea of filling his stomach with icy water. But he had to get away from there. He had to keep on walking, and the water might still help a little.

Chris bent down to the gently heaving surface and carefully, lest his face be kissed with cold, began to drink. Below, only inches from his eyes, another and smaller world swayed in the echoes from deeper water. In the ripple of shadow and light, grains of sand rolled slowly across the bottom. Bright flakes of mica gleamed like gold—how often they had deceived the boy—and then betrayed themselves by rising and soaring in that miniature sky.

It was into this restless and constantly changing place that another shadow moved. Chris saw it only vaguely at first but knew it was a fish curving away from deeper water. Hunting, or perhaps only wanting to rest, it slowly slipped in toward the shore.

He stopped drinking and backed off to watch. It moved a bit to the right, a little to the left, and came on with short, cautious flicks of its tail.

Chris held absolutely still, waiting for it to stop and hover. He not really thinking about it. If any thought passed through his mind, it was that of the bobcat and the ease with which it had caught a fish. Instinctively, rather than with any deliberation, he wanted to catch this one. It represented food, and in the panic of hunger, he once more ignored the question of cooking it.

Trembling, frightened by the importance of it, Chris suddenly plunged his hand in and grabbed for the fish. For an instant he even touched its silken side. But there was no grasping it, no reward of feeling it imprisoned and wriggling in his hand. In a wink, the fish was gone, and the boy went after it, scrambling through the rippling water on all fours to search frantically and blindly for what simply was not there anymore.

Chris stopped finally and, seeing his wild-eyed expression reflected in the water, stood up and hurried back to the warm sand. Shivering, he sat down to let the sun dry his clothes.

Perhaps headlong and unthinking flight had its own natural term, and therefore a time when it merely comes to an end. Again, it might have been the impact of seeing his own face caught in the last moment of frightened futility, or nothing more than the shock of cold water.

But whatever the reason, Chris had now begun to function. And the first indication of it was his admitting to himself that he could not go on.

How long could he last, if he did? How long before he dropped in his tracks, too weak to do anything except slip into dreams and die? He did not know. But soon enough.

No, he had to stop where he was. It was that simple.

Chris found it hard to look at the situation and

think of it as being simple. Beyond knowing the river flowed past his home, he was in every other sense lost in the wilderness.

He was hardly prepared for such a thing; not in those thin clothes and having nothing more than a small, broken-bladed pocket knife and a handkerchief. And yet, he had been carried far beyond that point where a grown man would go without a rifle and a packhorse heavily loaded with supplies. Even then, how many such foresighted adventurers were lost forever because of some unexpected treachery of nature?

Nevertheless, the overwhelming whole of his circumstance could be boiled down to two basic requirements which, if met, would allow him a reasonable expectation of living and reaching home. He needed to find food and, in some way or other, he had to stay warm at night.

Food had to be the first consideration; night was still in the distance. Chris looked around, not sure how to begin.

A little envious, he could not help thinking of the bobcat again, and how marvelously equipped it was. With claws and teeth, sharp senses, and an ability to move silently and swiftly, the cat needed only patience to live well in the forest.

But then the boy realized that it was wrong to think in terms of what that animal had for tools and what he, by comparison, did not have. The bobcat, after all, was not the only creature in the forest.

There were birds, and weasels, bears, squirrels, and mountain lions, deer, rabbits, and raccoons, skunks . . . the list was seemingly endless, and each species had its own way and its own rules for survival. And not all were predators. Nature was neither so haphazard nor accidental in its provisions. Wrens were not required to prey on rabbits, and rabbits did not feed on eagles.

The difference between these creatures and himself, therefore, was of little consequence. That he had never before needed to do anything but sit down at a table and eat what his mother put in front of him did not really matter.

The important thing here was *not* the admirable ability of the animals to feed themselves, but the fact that nature had provided them with food to eat!

Chris felt silly at coming to this conclusion, and almost grinned at himself. Of course, nature provided! How many times had he seen deer grazing in dew-wet meadows and hummingbirds hovering for a shimmering instant at the face of a flower? How often had he watched rabbits feeding in the shadowed edges of the clearing or, down at the river when the moon was bright, found raccoons engaged in the rather foolish chore of washing frogs?

He had known it all along, but he had not really thought about it until now because he had never needed to let nature provide for him.

Almost dry, and warm again, Chris began walking slowly along the river. The problem was still there. Where did he start? Meat was out of the question; it had to be caught and cooked. He could not follow the example of birds and eat insects, or even consider the fat grubs that bears and other animals loved to root for under decaying logs.

The boy could not picture himself feeding on grass, like the deer in the meadows. But then he stopped, realizing that such a notion was perhaps not so far from the truth. Grass, leaves, the roots of growing things; were they so different than the vegetables that Eric Holm grew in the clearing?

Chris looked at a clump of grass near his feet. It was that wiry and enduring kind that managed to survive both the long sleep of winter and the high, violent waters of spring.

He reached down to break off a blade, and crumpling it with all the haste of hunger, shoved it in his mouth to chew. The grass tasted bitter and dry and he quickly abandoned the idea. Disappointed, and nearly going on to look for something else, Chris remembered the possibility of roots.

The slender kind that grass put down, he supposed, would be easy to chew. Too, it seemed logical that the roots, not being green, would have a different taste.

Eager and full of hope, he got down and pulled a handful of it free. The roots, full of sand and dirt, did not look very promising. But, he tried to reassure himself, neither did turnips and potatoes until they were washed.

Chris went to the water and began rinsing them. When they were finally clean, the boy nibbled at the tender ends and found them rather tasteless and a little gritty. The roots were at least palatable, though, and it felt good to be chewing and swallowing something.

He had no way of knowing whether they were nourishing or not. One drawback, however, was immediately obvious, and that was the slowness of it. He supposed it would take most of the day, eating constantly, even to begin to blunt the edge of his hunger.

Chris washed two more clumps and moved on, watching for anything else that might supplement his meager diet.

It was not an altogether safe thing to be doing, tasting this and trying that. He had learned long ago to recognize those plants that made his skin itch and break out in bumps. Naturally, they could not be eaten. But there were others, harmless looking and perhaps even pretty, that could sicken and possibly kill. And, of all the many plants growing among the trees by the river, which were they? The animals knew and avoided them, and Chris wished he had paid more attention to this world instead of dreaming so much of other places. As it was, forced by the desperate need for food, he had to take the chance.

It was noon before Chris, slowly making his way upriver, met with any success.

He had reached a small, happily bubbling creek that fed into the river, and found on its opposite side a bed of familiar and delicate, water-filled plants. The stem came up to one round leaf, something like a lily, and he seemed to recall hearing his mother refer to it as Miner's Lettuce.

Whatever the name, he had found some satisfaction in its cool juices and pleasant green taste. It had more weight to it, and could be eaten faster, and so he stopped bothering with the roots.

Still, when the sun was gone, and evening crept between the mountains, Chris could not look back across the several miles he had covered and find one minute when hunger or weakness had not dogged his steps. Feeling neither better nor worse, he had done no more than hold his own.

He supposed he ought to be grateful for what little he had found to eat, but now he had to stop and turn to the other problem while there was still light enough to see.

Chris had decided, that afternoon, to spend the night away from the river. He remembered it being said that river air was damp, and that the cabin would have been built farther away if it had not been for the convenient water supply. How much difference it would make, he did not know; perhaps, in his case, none. But it was worth looking into, and he thought he would also try covering himself with pine boughs.

The boy worked his way up the slope toward the mountains and found a likely looking spot some two or three hundred yards from the water. Quickly, in the growing dark of the forest and in a freshening breeze, he went around to all the smaller pines whose branches were close to the ground.

It took time; the slender limbs were tough and springy and hard to break, but finally he had what looked like enough.

Gathering them in one place, he stretched out on the softly carpeted ground and, pulling the boughs over himself, settled down.

It did not work as he had hoped. There were not enough needles to fill all the air spaces. He could not pull it tightly around him as he would a quilt. No matter how the cover was arranged, the wind found its way in.

Chris kicked them off and sat up, feeling both disgusted and alarmed. Only his back had felt warm, and what was the value of that? For all his good intentions, the night had caught him again, unprepared! And maybe this was the night that would do it. . . .

Unavoidably, his thoughts returned to the joys of a fire; what a heaven-sent thing it would be if he could only find the secret of it and build one now!

He had read enough stories about Indians to know that a fire could be built without matches. Once he had pretended to be *Uncas* and, "camping" just beyond the edge of the clearing, tried rubbing two sticks together. But nothing came of it.

51

In his desperation Chris could not help trying it again. He found a length of dried pine and broke it in two. Grasping one piece by the end and bracing it with his feet, he took the other and rubbed with it as hard and fast as he could. The wood became hot to the touch, but no magic and glowing coal sprang into existence. Weak and trembling from the effort, he had to give it up.

There was another way. He remembered, vaguely, a short bow that turned a spindle and— What was the use! It was all wishful thinking.

Not wanting to see or feel what was coming in the forest's blue-black gloom, Chris sank down and pressed hard into the needles. He felt so helpless and exposed, and he could not understand why it had to be. He was a human being and supposedly more intelligent than the animals living out here. And yet they knew how to stay warm.

Even Griper, domesticated as he was, seemed to be smarter about such things. The boy remembered when Griper wandered off once and, caught by a blizzard, was gone for two days. He had worried, until his father explained how dogs dug into the snow and let themselves be buried until the storm was over. Away from the wind, their coats trapping body heat and keeping it from melting the snow, dogs could stay comfortably warm.

Chris stiffened suddenly, and pushed his fingers deep into the needles. Why not? *Of course it would work!*

Frantically, and almost with joy, he dug at the thick layer of needles until he had scooped out a place as long as he was and three or four inches deep.

Sitting in it, and beginning with his feet and legs, Chris raked the displaced needles back. When he was through, he was lying under a mound with only his head sticking out. It was itchy and full of prickles, but that discomfort could hardly matter. He was *warm!*

Watching the stars glittering in the treetops, he let weariness catch up with him and then closed his eyes.

From somewhere higher on the mountain, and almost lost in the song of pines, came a sound that caught him on the very border of sleep and made him smile.

Bears were quarreling up there. The big Cinnamons . . . short-tempered and heavy with autumn fat. He knew where he might find food tomorrow.

Chapter Six

Chris woke just before sunrise, that third day.
Hunger still raged within, and weakness clung to
his bones like some ravaging disease. It was not,
however, as bad as it could have been. He had
slept deeply and without dreams through all of the
long, bitter night. And bitter it had been, indeed.
His bed of needles became a matter of pride and
even greater satisfaction when he got up and discovered that the ground, between the sheltering
trees, was crisp with frost.

Only now was he cold, exposed to that morning
air, and if it had not been for the need to eat and
move on, the boy would have stayed under cover
until the sun came past the ridge.

Remembering the quarreling bears, Chris turned
and headed upward through the forest. It was a

steep and tiring climb. He would have preferred not to expend himself like that, and the possibility of running into a bear made him uneasy. Of course, those powerful beasts could be encountered anywhere, and because they were good fishermen, his homeward path along the river was no exception. It was, very simply, one thing to leave such meetings to chance and quite another to seek out a place where they had been heard so recently.

But it was a fact, and one which had not occurred to him before last night, that the bears were in their time of gorging. From the beginning of autumn, until snow began to fall, they ate constantly and greedily to acquire the heavy layer of fat that would nourish them during the long months of hibernation.

The boy knew very little about what bears ate. Out of curiosity or bent on thievery, and alarming his mother no end, they often came shuffling into the clearing. Those visits, however, had not taught him anything useful, and although he had encountered them in the forest on occasion, he never stayed around to observe what they were doing. But, of those parts of their diet he did know about, most were unfit for human consumption; the rest were hard to find, now, or impossible to attain.

He could not, for example, eat insects or the mice that bears spent patient hours digging out of dead and fallen trees. Chris was very fond of wild honey, but he did not have a bear's thick hide and coat to protect him against a swarm of furious bees. His father, when he found a bee-tree, always waited until the bees were deep in winter sleep before robbing them.

All considered, then, he knew his prospects of finding something to eat up above were not at all encouraging. Unfortunately, the greatest possibility was that they had quarreled over absolutely nothing. Bears were notoriously bad-tempered. At best, they might have fought over the right to a wintering place. But he could not, for a moment, ignore even the slightest chance of finding food.

Chris stopped to catch his breath, and then went on.

The thought that kept teasing him was that, although it was late in the year for such a thing, the bears *might* have found some kind of berry patch up on the mountain.

Those familiar to him, in the low-lying forest around the clearing, were gone now. Time and the creatures that fed on them had seen to that.

Still, nature was not at all that precise. High in the cooler air of the mountains, perhaps in shaded ravines where the sun touched only briefly, it was possible for a plant to be late in blooming and later still in coming to fruit.

As realistic as he tried to be, it was impossible not to feel some excitement as he climbed. If he did find edible berries up there, and if there were enough to fill all his pockets, he would be able to eliminate the worst of hunger for the next couple of days.

Yes! With something that substantial in his stomach, he could really start walking. Maybe two days of hard traveling would take him close enough to home so that it would not matter if he did not find anything else to eat.

It was perhaps an hour later that the forest grew thin and the steep slant of the ground turned level beneath his feet. Chris came out into the open and, stopping to rest, surveyed the scene before him.

He was well below the summit and that final, ragged line where timber stopped fighting the elements. But here, in the first of several high meadows, the mountain thrust its bones through browning and stunted grass. There were, here and there, tangles of ground-hugging and lifeless vine, and gray corpses of trees that had been downed by furious winds long ago.

It was not very hopeful.

Still trembling from the climb, Chris slowly walked across to the narrow line of trees separating that clearing from the one above it. When he came out the other side, the boy saw the same, unpromising desolation . . . and then, a little farther on, the ground sloping gently downward.

As he approached, ready to believe he had only wasted precious time and energy, the slope revealed itself to be perhaps thirty yards long, coming to an end in a dark and sheltered hollow below the next border of trees.

The sun was coming over the sunmit and shining in his eyes, and so it was not until he took a few steps downward that he realized the hollow was not merely deep in shade, but thick with vines and shrubs. And all around him now, were the unmistakable signs of bear. . . .

Satisfying himself that the beasts were no longer there, Chris hurried down into the hollow and began pushing his way through the growth.

Most of it came up to his middle, and some reached well over his head, lush in that catch-basin of rich soil. It was the bigger growth that obscured his vision and prolonged the search. But he remained patient. After all the climbing he had done, the berries just *had* to be there.

The boy reached one end of it, near a ledge of rock and a tumble of boulders, and turned to work back toward the other end. Yes, after climbing so far, and being so terribly hungry, he had to find what he was looking for . . . and he did.

Chris looked at them for several seconds, those incredible purple jewels, before he believed what he saw. Berries! Clusters of them were hanging from half a dozen red-stemmed plants about four feet tall. They were close to being gone; some had already begun to shrivel and dry, emphasizing how lucky he was to find them.

Lucky? The thought that they might be poisonous came to him then. But deciding he could eat them if bears could, Chris popped a few into his mouth and began to chew. To his dismay, they were terribly bitter and he had to swallow fast. Making a face over the lingering taste, and wishing for a drink of water, he learned very quickly to swallow them whole.

Two or three handfuls were sufficient to satisfy his hunger, and it did not surprise him; his stomach had done some shrinking in the last couple of days. It was a glorious feeling, however, to be full, and Chris went on to look for more.

He soon realized that the hollow was not going to yield the wealth of berries he had hoped to find. But if he only found enough for one or two meals, he could still travel pretty far before hunger stopped him again. As he searched, Chris decided the smart thing would be to ration them; save half for tomorrow and the rest for the next day. After that, with a reasonable distance behind him, he could better afford the time and energy needed for another search.

Chris stopped in his tracks, hearing a noise behind him, and knew even before he turned around that it was a bear! The morose and terrifying animal was back near the rock ledge, walking erect and coming toward him with its head down.

That posture signaled its intention to fight, and the boy wasted no time in scrambling out to open ground. He ran up the slope and heard, when he reached the top, the bear's tremendous bulk crashing through the undergrowth.

Knowing he had to be quick, Chris sprinted toward the nearest tree. For all its fat, the bear could still run as fast as a dog.

He did his best, with the bear's explosive breath sounding closer with every stride. Running felt like the glue-footed and hopeless thing it was in nightmares; it took forever to reach the tree, and forever all over again to grab a limb and start climbing.

The tree shuddered violently under the impact of the bear's weight, and Chris was certain the enraged animal was going to climb after him. When he was about fifteen feet up, the boy dared look down for the first time, and saw the bear standing below, watching him.

Out of breath and badly shaken, Chris settled down on a limb to rest. He was safe for the time being, anyway. The heavy fat that would keep the bear alive through the winter was also enough, he guessed, to keep it from climbing trees.

"Go on! Get away from here!" he yelled, hoping the bear would leave. Sometimes, back in the home clearing, that was all it took. But bears were unpredictable at best, and this big Cinnamon kept on looking up at him with red and piggish little eyes.

Finding a couple of pine cones within reach, Chris tried throwing them, and managed to hit his target both times. But this only served to irritate an already mean-tempered animal, and he decided to leave well enough alone. Sooner or later, the bear would tire of waiting and go back to its den, satisfied that the argument had been won.

Looking back at it now, Chris realized that that was all it was. The quarreling last night had not been over berries; there were so few. At the end of the hollow, somewhere in that jumble of rock under the ledge, was a snug and sheltered place in which a bear could hibernate until the spring thaw. This one had laid claim to it, and would challenge anything that came near.

Chris sat on the limb for more than an hour before the Cinnamon gave up and left. The bear slowly went back to the rim of the hollow, stood erect and watched him for a minute longer, and then was gone from sight.

The boy started down and, finding it difficult, could not understand how he had climbed the tree in the first place. Finally he made it to the ground and began the long walk to the river. It was all he could do. To return to the hollow and continue searching for berries was out of the question.

Somewhere below the meadows, maybe halfway to the river, Chris suddenly became sick and lost all that he had eaten. Weakened by it, and feeling feverish, he could only wonder about the berries. Was it because he had swallowed them whole, or had he eaten too fast after starving for so long? Were they poisonous after all?

Badly in need of water, he made himself go on. If the berries were seen again, there was just one way of answering the questions, and that was by eating them. For the time being, at least, it was not an experiment he wanted to consider.

By the time the river was in sight once more, the feeling of being sick was mostly gone, and Chris supposed it might be a matter of good fortune that he had stopped chewing the berries. If they were poisonous, he had not given them much of a chance to get into his system.

Thirsty and impatient, he came out of the forest and hurried toward the river's edge. He was startled to see a large black animal nosing wearily around in his footprints, a few yards downstream. Chris looked for a long time before he knew, before he realized that the poor, bedraggled-looking beast was *Griper!*

"Hey!" The boy shouted and ran toward him, and the Labrador turned and yelped joyously. But, in the middle of happiness and haste, there was a rock and a wrong way of stepping on it. Crying out, Chris collapsed in the sand and clutched at his ankle.

Griper was on him immediately, putting weariness aside and expecting to play and have his ears tugged. But Chris could only slap at that kind face until the dog retreated in hurt confusion. It could not be helped. The pain was blinding, filling his entire being until there was nothing else and the world was lost in a reddening haze. Even then, what it might mean was all too clear.

How was he going to *walk?*

Chapter Seven

Though it could stretch time in its grip and become seemingly endless, the pain finally began to subside. It was like slowly backing away from a hot and consuming fire until, weakened and feeling a little sick, he could begin to breathe again. Left with a thin sweat shining on his face, Chris crawled to the river and drank until he could hold no more. With great care, then, he eased the injured joint into the cold water and stared at it with frightened disbelief.

Had it been a wrist, or an elbow, there would at least have been no question about walking. This way— The boy did not like thinking about it. Why did it have to be his ankle! What had he done to it?

Except for a little swelling, the ankle did not

look bad. But the way it throbbed and ached was something else. He supposed it could be just a bad twist that would delay him for only a few hours. Chris knew it might also be broken.

A broken bone—he groaned at the idea—would have him on a crutch for all the miles remaining. Indeed, with that kind of handicap, he was not even sure the journey was possible.

In the best of circumstances, which meant having enough to eat, good weather, and not running into unexpected problems, he might conceivably make fifteen or twenty miles a day.

The question of food, however, was yet to be solved. If he had to be satisfied with Miner's Lettuce and roots, he would do well to cover ten miles between each dawn and dark. Add to that a broken ankle and a crutch— Well, what else could it mean? Days might turn into weeks, he told himself, and he did not have that much time. Winter was close now.

Chris glanced worriedly skyward, almost expecting to find ominous clouds drifting between him and the sun. The air was empty and blue, and yet it was as if the high crying of southing geese still lingered with urgent warnings.

He shuddered and began to weep. So much was at stake! The difference, between a broken ankle and one that was not, could very well be the same as that between life and death. And which was it going to be? All he had to do, to learn the truth, was try bending it.

The boy wiped his eyes and looked at the swollen joint. He was afraid to find out. In not knowing, there was always a chance left, and a little hope. The instant he tightened his muscles and tried, that would be it. Good or bad, the alternative would be gone.

But to put it off was wrong, and Chris knew it. Time simply was not going to stop just because he was afraid. Broken bones or otherwise, he still faced the necessity of finding food, and miles had to be covered whether he walked unhindered or at the pace of a log-crawling beetle. There was no way of avoiding it, and who could know beforehand the meaning of a single, wasted hour?

Reluctantly Chris pulled his leg from the water and, bracing it behind the knee with his hands, held the ankle in the air. He did not like the look of it, but maybe the whiteness and wrinkles from the long soaking only made it seem worse than before.

"The toes," he said aloud. "First, the toes."

Griper, hearing his voice coming in softer tones, approached cautiously.

"Come on. It's all right. I'm sorry."

Chris stroked the dog's massive head, seeing now how thin and footsore he was. It was a grim clue to the distance ahead. How far, was still the river's secret. But it was no secret that a dog, settling into a steady and patient trot, could cover a good many miles in a day. The boy knew that Griper would have had to rest occasionally, and he *might* have holed up somewhere during the dark and cold of the long nights. Even so, there was no ignoring the fact that the Labrador had been following the river for more than *two and a half days*. . . .

Unhappily, the boy gave Griper one more pat and said, "Now sit. I have to find out about my ankle. Sit!"

The dog did as he was told, and the boy lifted his foot from the water again.

It took a while to reach down through stiffened muscles and produce a result. His foot had become almost without feeling in that icy water, and when the toes did move, it was as if they were not really a part of him. But, encouraged, the boy cautiously turned his attention to the ankle.

Slowly, almost imperceptibly, he worked the front of his foot up, and then down. Chris sucked in his breath, and just as carefully bent the foot to the left, to the right, and back again. There was pain, but not sharp and stabbing as he had anticipated.

Growing more confident, he worked the joint a little more quickly, and still nothing happened. Chris returned it to the water and stretched out, not knowing whether to laugh or cry.

Griper seized the opportunity to wash the boy's face and would not be stopped. But, sloppy as it was, Chris could have not cared less. There did not seem to be any broken bones! He could not jump

up and run around just yet, but his ankle apparently was all right.

Trying his weight on it later, Chris found his ankle a good deal better. Time and cold water were doing their work. But it would slow him down that afternoon, and he supposed the tenderness would remain for a day or two. Although it was not something that called for a crutch, he did see the value of using a walking stick for a while.

The nearest supply of wood, light and easy to cut, was a stand of willow just a few yards upstream. Chris limped to it, and, finding a straight piece an inch thick and five feet long, got out his pocket knife and went to work cutting it free.

He carried it to the water, where he sat down to soak his ankle some more, and began stripping off the branches. Griper collapsed in a heap nearby and, with a great, gusty sigh, was asleep. Chris watched, feeling an immense gratitude. The dog could neither speak nor lessen the distance ahead. But no matter what the miles held, he no longer had to face them alone.

The boy returned to his task, removing the branches and peeling the bark away from clean, white wood. It was in the middle of this that he saw another fish coming from deep water to hover in a shaft of sunlight.

With pain no longer burying it, hunger returned with that fish to dominate his every thought. It mattered little that he still had no way of cooking anything; the trout tantalized him, and he swore he could eat one raw if given the opportunity.

Chris was tempted to jump in after it, but he was in no condition for that, and, as he had already discovered, catching a fish with one's hands was very nearly impossible.

"Griper!" he whispered and shook the dog awake. The big retriever got up and stood beside him, and Chris pointed at the water. "Look at it, boy! A fish!"

The dog, trying hard to understand, only looked at the finger and the notion came to nothing. Chris let him go back to sleep; he supposed it was not likely that Griper could have done anything about it anyway. He looked at the fish and then at the walking stick with growing frustration. If only he had a hook and line!

There were other ways, he knew. From his father he had heard about nets and harpoons, and single lines that bore clusters of baited hooks. In Lousiana's geography lessons and his own reading, Chris had discovered people who fished with baskets, cormorants, or drove fish before them into traps with nothing more than their bare, churning feet. Among these methods, there had to be one he could use. But what?

A net made from the wiry river grass and tied to the end of his stick was one possibility. Too, the slender lengths of willow that he had trimmed off the stick were the kind that could be woven into a basket. That sort of thing took a lot of labor, though, and he could not really picture the quick and wary trout holding still long enough to be scooped from the water.

The only thing left that he could consider was a spear. A *spear* . . . Chris hefted the stick and wondered if he had not hit on the best idea.

With no small amount of excitement, he removed the last of the bark. By then the trout was gone, but it was not important. There were a lot of fish in the river.

Now he had to concentrate on fashioning his weapon, and at first he did not see it as anything more than a sharp stick to be thrown. But then it occurred to him that throwing a spear required considerable skill and, once thrown, a means for retrieving it; he had neither. Remembering how a fish fought and struggled, he saw that a simple point was not going to be enough. There had to be some way of keeping his catch from jumping off.

There was only one alternative. Instead of throwing the spear, he would have to jab with it. And rather than depend on one point, he decided to make two by splitting the end. A small stone could be used to hold the points apart at a slight angle, and a strip of bark wrapped tightly around, above and below the stone, would keep the split from deepening.

It took very little time to complete. In less than an hour Chris had his weapon, and he was proud of it; doubly so because he still had, by inverting it, the needed walking stick.

Cautiously testing his ankle, and finding he was able to move around without too much trouble, the boy woke his dog and went along the edge of the water looking for fish.

The river was full of them; a fisherman would never need to strain his patience there. The only problem Chris faced in that respect was finding fish where he could get close enough to use the spear.

For the most part the river was too deep. And where it was not, the currents were still swift; in that brightness of water fish became as elusive as quicksilver. It was not really out of choice, then, that he decided to work those frequently encountered shallows where the water was quiet and clear.

Fortunately, fish did come to them seeking fallen insects, and they seemed to enjoy resting on those warmer bottoms. Just as important, some of the pools were studded with rocks that could be used as stepping stones.

It was not, of course, as simple as all that. Griper had to be scolded twice before he stopped plunging through the shallows after him. But even when he saw a fish and went by himself, balancing precariously from one stone to the next, his quarry invariably took fright and flicked out of reach. Chris finally learned it was better to go out and, standing absolutely still, wait for fish to appear.

Being in the right place at the right time, Chris as last got his chance. A nice fat one came in lazy, searching turns and hovered less than three feet away. Ever so slowly, moving no more conspicuously than a sapling stirring in the wind, he bent down and aimed the spear.

With pounding and anxious heart, the boy suddenly made his thrust, and the fish was gone! In a wink, it just was not there anymore. And it puzzled him. If his senses were to be trusted, he could almost swear that the spear had passed right through the fish . . . as if that fish, like some phantom, had no substance! It was nonsense, of course. Just the same, he could not discard the feeling that his target had not been where it appeared to be.

Seeing a small stone sitting on the bottom, and using the walking-end so as not to blunt his points, Chris shoved the spear toward it and touched empty sand; the stone was several inches closer than where he was aiming.

The illusion was beyond his understanding, but if he was going to succeed, it was obvious he would have to disregard what his eyes told him and aim below the target.

Chris made his way back to shore and, planning to return to the last place and try again, hesitated. The loss of time and distance bothered him. He made it a rule, then and there, always to move upstream. No matter what he was looking for or trying to do, each step had to count toward his getting home.

Twice more he tried to get a fish, and then the day was done. Chris found and ate some Miner's Lettuce; it did a little to satisfy him, and interested Griper not at all. The boy tried and tried again to get him to eat, and the retriever just as patiently refused. It worried him. Going by appearances, at least, Griper had not found anything to eat during his long trip downriver. But there was nothing more to be done except head for higher ground. As it was, darkness had already come to the forest when he scooped out a bed for the dog, covered him, and then did the same for himself.

Perhaps, he thought, tomorrow would be better. With luck, he would feel the weight of a trout on the end of his spear. But, for now at least, it seemed like a losing battle. After all his trying, he was still hungry and growing weaker.

His failure made the night seem darker, and the world where he was lost became twice as big.

Thoughts of home were all he had to comfort him, and Chris reached for them, lovingly. Although he was warm, it was warmth without cheer, and so he thought of the hearth and its happy blaze. He saw himself standing with his back to it; his father and mother sat there, silent in their contentment, and . . . yes, Griper had to be there too. That silly hulk . . . he had earned his name early in life by complaining about every small creature that entered or intruded on *his* clearing. The complaints had yet to end. Even now, as he pictured him, the Labrador slept with a suspicious nose pointed toward the door.

Chris drifted closer to sleep. It was a pleasant scene, enough to made him sigh and smile a little, and he guarded it as carefully as he would a candle from the wind.

Chapter Eight

He heard a fish twice, its fins breaking the quiet surface of the shallows. Although it happened under the brightening sky of morning and no more than a few feet away, he could not see anything. Night and the river had conspired to hide, with thick and wisping fog, that world of water and sand. It held to the ground, rising no higher than his knees.

Chris was disappointed and impatient. Aside from his desire to get home, he wanted a fish more than anything else. He wanted it *now*, and nature seemed bent on playing games; there had not been a fog before.

Nothing would be accomplished, though, by standing around and fussing. The fog simply was not going to vanish until the air turned warmer.

"We might as well spend the time walking," he told Griper and, limping slightly, went back to higher ground at the edge of the forest. The fog was not as bad there.

Each step he took diminished his journey. The boy knew the value of taking a step and never having to take it again. But hunger robbed his spirit, and an hour found him covering one slow mile.

He encountered Miner's Lettuce here and there, eating it grudgingly. How could that slight, water-filled weed compare with the dreamed-of fish? Still, with the fog persisting, it was better than nothing. And in watching for that plant, Chris discovered another.

He had stepped on it, breaking the stem, and his sharpened sense of smell caught a familiar scent. It was only vague, almost lost in the cool air, and he went a step or two beyond before he realized what it was.

"Wild onion!"

Turning around, he dropped to his knees and found it. There was not much left. Time and frost had done their work, and so he could not eat the part that was above the ground. The onion itself, however, was intact and waited just below the surface for spring to come again.

Chris pulled it out and, ignoring the dirt cling-ing to the bulb, ate it greedily. The taste was strong and bitter, and nearly made his eyes water. Still it was food and, though no bigger than a marble, more substantial than the greens he had been eating.

Looking anxiously around, he found fourteen more. Trimmed of their dead stems, they barely filled the palm of his hand. It was a windfall just the same, and he was exceedingly grateful to have them.

Remembering the dog, he held out a few. Griper only sniffed at them, sneezed, and turned away.

"But you've eaten onions in leftovers!" Chris protested and, then, finding no pleasure in it, said, "All right. That much more for me."

The big question was whether to eat them all now or save some for later. Which would do him the most good? Chris wanted to eat them all at once, with the idea that there would be more as he went along. But there was no guarantee that what grew here could be found again often enough to be counted as a regular supply of food.

He remembered a rule that his father had made. "For every six logs you cut for winter," Eric said, "cut a seventh for the spring that might be late." There was no lesson in it here, save that of caution. And so he ate half, pocketed the rest, and the two went on their way.

The ground fog burned off shortly after that, and Chris had one opportunity to spear a fish, and failed. Above that point, he stopped finding the shallow pools. The river was faster here, and deeper, and from somewhere not far upstream its voice came rumbling like imprisoned thunder.

It was, of course, that part of the river that had stormed and raged at him so furiously, and where the raft began breaking up.

Their path soon slanted upward in a steep climb and, leveling off, led along the rim of that narrow-walled and tortured place. Having passed this way on foot once before, Griper showed no interest in it, but cautiously stayed away from the edge. Chris, on the other hand, was drawn to it out of grim fascination. How had he managed to survive such a place? It was incredible! Breathing, full of hunger and feeling the trembling earth beneath his feet, he was his own proof that a raft could and did negotiate that watery inferno. But it was still hard to think of it as being possible.

After a half-mile or less, the twisting chasm widened, became less deep, and then was behind them with nothing more than hastening water to hint of its existence.

The sun was directly overhead when he came again to a pool of quiet water. A single rock broke the surface near the center of the shallows. While Griper waited, washing his paws and resting, Chris waded out to it. His feet roiled the bottom and, he supposed, disturbed any fish that might be around; it was not a good way to begin. But he was tired now, and quite willing to kneel there and do nothing for a while. The miles covered that morning had not been easy.

It was a relief to stare into the water, letting his

eyes go out of focus until he no longer saw the bottom or knew the changing quality of sunlight there. He had simply put the world aside to go somewhere else.

Into that peaceful and uncaring interval the fish came swimming as slowly as the passing minutes, came flickering to the edge of vision more like a remembered wish than reality, and when he awakened to the fact of it, almost startled, Chris felt as if he had been sleeping.

It happened too quickly for him to get excited, or for anxiety to grow and become what the hunters around Bodwin's Landing called "buck-fever." All at once the fish was *there,* and moving slowly by, and the boy did not have time to do anything but aim and plunge his spear into the water.

The force of the thrust threw him off balance, and Chris pitched forward into the shallows. Frantically, he found his knees and stood up to gasp for air. For that one hectic moment, strangling on the water he had swallowed, the boy was not aware of anything else. But when the moment passed, and he was able to breathe freely again, Chris suddenly realized that he was still holding on to the spear and that it was inexplicably heavier than before . . . yes, and jumping in his hands as if alive! Crying out and startling Griper into a fit of deep-throated barking, Chris swung the spear skyward. He had done it! *He had his fish!*

Stumbling blindly ashore, he pulled the fish off

and placed it on a flat stone so that he could admire and wonder at it.

Griper went for it, drooling, and Chris clouted him across the nose. "Stop it! You just wait a minute!" The dog backed off, but not very far, and the boy went back to admiring his prize. The trout was a fine one, sleek and fat, measuring perhaps fifteen inches.

Chris sat down beside it, knowing all the joy and triumph of one who has just won a victory. And there was pride, too, the pride of having discovered he could provide for himself.

"Ain't you a beauty," he whispered to it. "A real beauty! Ain't he something, Griper? Just look at it!"

The dog did not need to be told to look. Indeed, he could do nothing else, and Chris decided it was not fair to keep his companion waiting any longer. But it did seem almost a shame to spoil the fish's graceful symmetry and reduce it to a mere piece of meat.

Getting out his knife and sharpening the broken blade a little on the stone, Chris cleaned the fish as he had seen his mother do so many times. He gave Griper the head and tail, entrails, and half of the meat. The rest he took down to the water to rinse.

The only thing it needed now, he thought, was to be dipped in flour and dropped into a frying pan, and it would be as good as anything Louisa Holm had ever put on the table.

Griper came looking for more, and the boy said, "You behave yourself! This is my share!"

Chris squatted, holding the meat across his palms, and frowned. The flour was not important, and a frying pan was not so much more convenient than a green, forked stick as to be indispensable. But not having a fire was something else again, and he remembered his hungry vow to eat a fish raw if and when he ever caught one.

Now that the fish was an accomplished fact, he was neither so sure nor quite as brave.

With the dog looking on, anxiously, the boy stared at it for a long time, and took even longer to peel a bit of the skin back and cut a piece of meat no bigger than his little finger. That, too, Chris examined with great care, as if just looking could tell him that the taste would be all right and that there was no real difference between cooked and raw meat.

Caution only made it worse. The longer he waited, the harder it became. Finally, and impulsively, he closed his eyes and hurriedly popped the bit of fish into his mouth.

Chris gagged on it immediately, and had to spit it out. The meat had not been in his mouth long enough to taste, really, and its consistency was no different than that of stewed chicken. But it was, unavoidably, *raw*.

At first, in his disappointment, Chris tried to minimize the importance of it. To have a belly full of strength-giving meat, he told himself, was all very well. But why act as if the fish were the only food in the world? Had he not dined on onions that morning? And did he not have seven left to eat at day's end?

Ought to be grateful, he thought. It's a lot better than you've been doing.

Nevertheless, disappointment and the feeling of defeat persisted; all his quiet arguing came to nothing. Catching a fish and being unable to eat it was like finding a dollar that could not be spent.

After a long drink of water Chris stuck the fish on his spear; he started out along the river.

To his sudden distress, Griper did not take his usual place in front, but fell in behind, silently watching the meat. The boy supposed he ought to give it to the dog. Wishing would not make it more palatable, and to keep what he himself could not eat was wrong. But . . . Chris bit his lip and tried not to notice. However useless to him, the fish represented hard-won food, and he could not bring himself to give it away.

Chris came awake in the dark and, seeing the deep brilliance of stars above the trees, tried to go back to sleep again. Dawn had not come, and there was neither sound nor scent of it in the air. Only a gentle wind stirred high in the pines.

And yet . . .

It was as if he could hear soundless things, and sense motion though his eyes were closed. Chris took a deep breath and, deciding it was his imagination, tried to get more comfortable. But the instant he moved, there was an angry chirring sound and the spear fell across him.

Griper came exploding out of his bed, his deep voice sounding the alarm; he circled twice and charged off into the night. Chris, at the same instant, sat up and grabbed at the spear. It was already too late. The fish was gone and he knew the thief by its sound and audacity. Only a raccoon would dare approach where dog and human slept. And with ring-tail and masked face, how dressed for the part it was!

Griper's barking, sounding halfway to the river, stopped after a while; it was a long time after that before the big retriever came back.

Cold and shivering, Chris crawled over and covered his companion again. As he returned to his own bed and settled into it, he could not help wondering what had happened to the fish. The boy felt some resentment over the possibility that Griper had eaten the meat instead of bringing it back. But he had to ask what difference it made, when he could not eat it himself; Griper was hungrier than the raccoon.

Still, the food was gone and the lesson was a hard one. He had learned a little too late that he competed with not only time and distance, but also the creatures that lived in the forest. They, like himself, were constantly searching for food.

Why had he been so careless? He could clearly remember the times his father had hung a newly smoked ham from a front-porch rafter. Yes, and tied it high enough so that nothing could get at it during the night.

Chris closed his eyes, unhappily looking for sleep. *Ham* . . . the word stayed, with all its delicious connotations, and made him remember something else.

Two years ago, several weeks before Thanksgiving, Eric Holm had gone to the Landing to buy a goose. The trip was made early so there would be time to fatten the bird, and because there was no guarantee of getting through later on. Snow often came before the holiday, sometimes with a fury that made travel impossible.

He had reached what Eric called the respectable age of eleven—"very close to needing a razor"— and the task of feeding the goose fell to him.

It was no small matter to open the crate and lower a pan of corn, bread scraps, and whatever else Louisa thought was good. It took a lot of dexterity to avoid being nipped painfully by that mean and hissing bird.

His father's face, shaped early by sea and wind and fierce winter, was that of Vikings. And yet somehow it managed to assume an almost absurd innocence when, after a week had passed, Eric asked, "Learn anything about geese?"

"What you thought I'd learn, I think," Chris remembered telling him, and his father, having been discovered in his joke, had laughed with more than the usual gusto.

The strange part of it was that he became fond of the goose. In spite of its bad temper and stupidity, there was something proud in that bird. It was also handsome.

And so it was that pleasant anticipation turned to gloom. He remembered thinking of the approaching holiday, not as a time of gracious festivity, but as a day of execution.

Protesting to his parents accomplished nothing. They only reminded him that he had never objected to eating the chickens they raised. Why was the goose so different?

The logic of it was undeniable. Just the same, he had gone out on the eve of Thanksgiving, while they were asleep, and turned the bird loose.

As expected, there was quite an uproar the next morning. Louisa was upset and disappointed, and it was not easy to sit down after his father, lapsing into Norwegian expletives, got through with him. But they ate ham that afternoon.

After dinner was over, and in a quieter, more reflective mood, Eric had tried to make a lesson of the whole episode.

Kindness, he said, and a respect for life whether it be ants or elephants, was a praiseworthy thing. It was not sensible, though, to buy a goose to eat and then let it wander off.

"You didn't save the bird's life, Chris."

"What do you mean?" he remembered asking. "You didn't get to chop its head off!"

Eric had smiled. "No. But it was a farm goose,

boy. It couldn't defend itself against a wild animal for long. You can be sure something got it before morning."

While the thought was not pleasant, it did not matter as much as he might have expected. Somehow it was more acceptable for the goose to die that way. Anything was better than eating what he had come to regard as a pet and, if nothing else, he had at least *tried*.

But he had thought only of the goose and himself, and not about the rest of what his father had tried to tell him. Perhaps it was not a lesson that could truly be learned when food was plentiful and easily had.

Not until now, desperately hungry and far from home, did he realize how wasteful he had been. What he remembered was two years in the past. And yet, in a sense, it was only minutes ago. Careless, wasteful . . .

Yes, the fish, like the walking goose, was gone.

Chapter Nine

The fifth day had only just begun, and Chris had walked less than a quarter of a mile when he found and speared his second fish. It came about so quickly and easily that, had it not been for the surprise in his face, he might have looked for the moment like some young and knowing savage. Chris did not, however, concern himself for long with the question of luck or growing skill. Last night's carelessness had been wiped away. If he could just find the courage to eat, much would be gained.

Chris cleaned and halved the fish as before and, after feeding the impatient dog, washed his own share in the river. When that was done, he put the meat on a rock and sat down beside it. But then all resolve melted away and left him helpless; the boy did not even want to look at it.

It baffled him. Chris thought about yesterday and how he had carried the fish around without any honest intention of trying again to eat it. Only when an enterprising raccoon had taken the meat did he begin to reconsider its importance. Supposedly a lesson had been learned, and now he found himself starting the same foolishness all over again.

The situation confronting him had not changed in the slightest. Home was far away, and to reach it he had to eat, protect himself from the elements, and walk. If the requirements were not met, death would come as certainly as the fall of the night. How, then, could he balk at the idea of eating a little meat?

"What's so hard about it? Go on! Look at it!"

Chris turned to face the fish. He knew it was not dirty, or anything like that. The trout had spent its life swimming in bright, clear water. Its carcass did not gape at him with infestations of rot and decay; the meat was pure and plump, and had about it only the stigma of being raw. And what was *raw* as opposed to *cooked* but a matter of simple taste?

Surely the difference was not so much greater here than it was between, for example, a baked apple and one that was eaten beneath the tree where it fell.

His reasoning seemed sound enough, and Chris finally dared cut a piece. He watched the river, as if to convince himself further that what he was doing was not unusual, and put the meat in his mouth.

The desire to spit it out was sudden and strong. He fought it back and made himself examine the experience more closely.

All right, he thought, it doesn't taste good. But it isn't killing you, either. Swallow and get another piece!

It took a long time to get it down, and a longer time to brace up to repeating the act. The second time around, Chris swallowed quickly and took a drink of water to wash away the taste. A few of those wild onions, he decided, would have been a big help at this point.

A precedent had been established, though, and that was the important thing. Two pieces had been eaten, and while the accomplishment certainly did not make the process a pleasant one, neither would it ever again be quite as hard.

Chris managed to consume nearly half of the meat before his rebellious stomach warned and made him stop. He put the remainder back on the spear, jammed the latter upright in the sand, and walked around until he was sure of keeping what he had gained.

Then, full of real food for the first time, the boy collapsed by the spear in drowsy triumph. He nearly fell asleep before he remembered last night's mistake; raccoons would not be a problem in the bright light of day, but Griper was something else.

"Lie down." He tugged at the Labrador until he obeyed. "You're a good dog, but I can't trust you with that fish."

Putting his arm around Griper's neck, Chris closed his eyes and slept. The problem of hunger had been conquered.

Griper was asleep and the sun high when Chris stretched and sat up. The way he felt surprised him. Much of the accustomed weakness had gone, and new strength flowed through his body. It was as if a heavy weight had been lifted from him.

Thus encouraged, he rinsed and chilled the last of the fish and then sat down to eat. He did not have to force himself this time.

When that was done, Chris woke the dog, took the spear and almost trotted between forest and river. It was his first opportunity really to cover ground, and he intended to make the most of it. His ankle no longer bothered him and, with a full stomach, he saw no reason why he could not keep on going for a while after sundown.

The evenings were short because of the sky-covering mountains. They would add only a mile or so to the day's walk before it became too dark to see, but he had to walk *hard,* and not one, single step taken along the course of the river could be dismissed as being unimportant.

And who could say? By not stopping to fish or hunt for food, and not taking time to rest until it was time to sleep, by making this best of days one hard push for all it was worth . . . well, who could say that tomorrow would not find home just beyond the next mountain?

"And what if it isn't?"

He stopped short. It was as if someone else had put the words in his mouth. Griper came back, panting and wagging his tail. Chris kneeled down to put his arm around the dog. He listened to the river's rushing and watched the quietly moving trees. It all seemed to say, *how foolish you are, Christian Holm.*

It was fine, this wanting to reach out and cover as many miles as the day would hold. There was no harm in hoping that tomorrow would find him near home. But to abandon caution, to slip into a false sense of well-being just because hunger was no longer there to emphasize the dangers, was as bad as being caught in the full cry of panic.

He had to go on gathering food at every opportunity, whether he needed it or not, simply because there was no way of knowing when it might cease to be available. Suppose, Chris told himself, there already had been a snow far to the north in the last couple of days. What if the snow was heavy, and then had been hit by a warming Chinook? The river could rise and turn angry, and there would not be any fishing for a while.

Just as important was the need to settle down to a sensible pace—one that could be maintained until nightfall. Chris knew now that if he had kept on the way he started out, he would have exhausted himself long before the day was over.

Taking a deep breath, and feeling the frustration of having to be patient, the boy shouldered his spear and once more began walking northward through the wilderness.

Twilight was only minutes old when Chris and Griper turned away from the river and wearily looked for a place to sleep.

Chris felt some disappointment in failing to spear another fish. Having found a few onions for himself, he was more concerned about Griper's welfare than his own. But neither of them were starving, and there was satisfaction in looking back at the distance covered. Home, Chris guessed, was perhaps fifteen miles closer.

Nevertheless, a new problem had arisen, forcing him to stop even though it was not yet too dark to travel. The soles of his feet felt as if all the skin had been worn away.

It was not something he had anticipated. Every year, when the days turned warm, he started going barefoot. His feet always became pretty tough with the passing months.

But even Griper was footsore from his journey downriver and the distance covered since. His own feet, then, could not be expected to take the punishment of so many miles. The terrain constantly changed along the river. While some of the walking was on soft forest floor, he just as often found himself on sand and stones, or moving through ankle-deep grass that hid all kinds of things to jab, saw, and scrape at his feet.

Chris found a place for them to sleep, beneath an ancient pine, and dropped to his knees to scoop the needles away.

He did not pause, afterward, to examine the damage, but got into the hollow and covered himself. It was too dark to see the blisters and bruises, covered as they were by dirt and sticky smears of pine pitch, and it did not much matter. He had looked two or three hours ago, when the soreness first began to be really noticeable. That it spelled trouble did not need confirming a second time. The boy could only hope that eleven or twelve hours of being off his feet would find them in better shape.

Chris watched the glittering heavens through the trees and remembered sadly that it was always about this time of year that he got his new boots.

On the last two trips to Bodwin's Landing, before the snows came, they purchased all their winter supplies. The hundred-pound sacks of grain and flour were loaded on the wagon then, along with canned goods, kerosene, and cartridges for the rifle—all the necessities that they could not, out of their own ingenuity or in the rich soil of the clearing, produce themselves. Having to last four or five months, it made an impressive pile. And among these things were the boots to replace the pair he had outgrown the spring before.

The first thing he did in that prideful moment of getting the boots home, Chris recalled, was rub them with neat's-foot oil until they were soft, pliable, and thoroughly waterproofed.

Although they were made of mere leather and rubber, there was in the first wearing a certain and undeniable sorcery. In those minutes of heavy-footed newness, striplings became men and small fry were giants; one prideful step could conquer a mountain, and surely all the beasts of the forest raised their heads and trembled at the sound of it.

Chris sighed and closed his eyes. What did it matter? Even his old pair, misshapen and worn, would have been a luxury and magic enough. He wished he had them now.

Chapter Ten

The big retriever was already up and nosing around the stand of pines when Chris pushed away the covering needles. Shivering in the glacial air of morning, he stood up and took a few worried steps. He wanted very badly to discover himself able to go on, and to make every hour of the day count toward getting home. It was difficult not to cheat a little, not to walk with exaggerated care and then, even on that soft duff beneath the pines, tell himself his feet were better. But, in truth, they would not have taken him half a mile.

Of course, the night's rest had helped some. The broken blisters and the skinned, raw places were not as full of fire as they had been. Time was good medicine and, indeed, the boy supposed if he stayed put for a couple of days his feet would heal completely.

The trouble was, he could not stay that long, and unless home was only a day's march away, it would not solve anything. Another day like yesterday, Chris knew, would find him facing the same problem all over again.

With Griper leading, he picked his way carefully down to the river and, after drinking, sat back to consider his predicament. The only solution to it, obviously, was that very item he had lacked in the first place—something to wear on his feet.

He was beginning to realize more with each passing day that the wilderness provided for those who knew where to look and how to take what they needed. But where in its remarkable scheming was there a pair of shoes for him?

Griper, who had trotted a few yards upstream, came back almost impatiently and stood looking at him.

"I know, boy. It's time to go, but I can't. Not yet."

It was all very well, he decided, to think about animal skins, and making use of them the way the Indians had. There was nothing mysterious about it. Given the chance to experiment a little, Chris knew he could probably devise a trap of some kind and catch a rabbit or raccoon. It would not be hard to make a better spear and, in time, learn how to throw it.

Yes. In *time* . . .

Chris bitterly picked up a stone and, throwing, watched it splash and disappear in the current.

It made better sense to tear strips of cloth from his pants and shirt, and tie them around his feet. But he had little enough to wear as it was, and did not want to do it unless there was absolutely no alternative.

The boy looked around at the trees, the various shrubs and plants; they were all that were left to him to consider.

Wood? Wooden shoes like a Hollander's? The idea had definite possibilities, and for a moment it was amusing to think how his parents would react to them. But he had to give it up. There would be too much carving involved, not to mention having first to cut through a rather large limb in three separate places just to get the material.

The notion of twisting river-grass into soft ropes and wrapping them around his feet occurred to him. Such a thing might work. He also had a feeling something might be done with slender willow branches—a miniature version of the snowshoe, perhaps. But grass was not durable, and the willow branch idea needed studying before he could decide one way or the other.

His eyes fell on a stand of birch, and at first he did not associate it with anything other than the fact that he remembered reading about birch-bark canoes. Then it struck him.

Any kind of bark that was solid, tough, and reasonably flexible . . . it almost *had* to work!

While it could not be expected to hold up like good boot-leather, Chris had a feeling if would last long enough to be practical. And whatever its other virtues, it was at least in constant supply.

Chris limped over to the birches and got out his knife. There was no need to stop and work out a plan first. Feet were feet, and what he needed was quite clear to him. It took only a few minutes to cut and peel two cylinders almost as big around as his feet and about ten inches long.

Slipping them on, he marked and trimmed away the excess. The open ends were a problem; there was nothing to keep sand and pebbles out. The boy soon discovered, however, that by making two slits in each end, flaps could be bent upward to close off the openings. These he tied in place with slender strips of green willow.

All that remained, then, was to fasten the shoes more securely to his feet and give them a try. For each, he ripped two strips of cloth from his handkerchief. Passing them through holes punched in the bark, he crossed the strips over the ankles and tied them at the front and back.

Standing up and taking a few experimental steps, he was delighted. "Look at me, Griper! I've got *shoes!*"

Chris walked a little more; the shoes felt stiff and awkward, but they protected his feet and he supposed he had only to get used to them.

Yes, he thought. He could travel now.

Although the opportunity presented itself two or three times, it was not until early afternoon that he was able to spear a fish and put an end to the hunger and weakness he and the dog were feeling again.

Having covered perhaps eight or ten miles by then, Chris was tired and would have welcomed an hour's rest; the dog too, he supposed. But the shoes were working well, and his feet were taking the distance better than expected. And so he went on, driven by the need to get home.

Home . . . it seemed like little more than a dream now. After nearly a week of knowing nothing but rolling water and wind, of seeing only mountains and endless forests, it was hard to remember exactly what it was like to sleep in a bed or hear the sound of a human voice. For the life of him, Chris could not recall the taste of hot stew and apple pie without exaggerating beyond belief.

It was almost as if Griper and that unending wilderness were the only realities. The cabin and the clearing, the people who lived there, might have been merely illusions like the cities and ships, the fabled ports of call he used to dream about, listening to the river.

Chris looked up through the trees toward the ridge, wanting badly to climb and see if the home mountains were visible. But he was certain he had yet to cross the distance seen from the mountainside on the first day. And whether they were in sight or not, he would get home a lot sooner if he did not waste time and energy on side trips.

Nearly a week? The boy stretched his legs and quickened the pace. Surely it was longer than that.

Chapter Eleven

Chris, had he been awake, would have seen bright stars caught and swimming in inky vapor, and then, like divine fireflies flashing for the last time, drowning in a bottomless dark. Had he not slept through those moments of sudden change, the boy would have heard wind rising on the ridges and sweeping downward across the forest with the sound of distant seas. And with it, almost lost in the hiss of bending pines, the muffled drumming of rain.

The squall had passed when Chris awoke. Its gusting had died, and only dark rain was left. Beneath the pine's scented canopy, the rain took longer to find him, and he did not stir until the first random drops found a way through and, cold, fell to strike his face.

Darkness became deeper for it, the world an empty and more lonely place; even the presence of Griper, sleeping no more than a foot away, did nothing to lessen the gloom.

At home, it had always been a pleasant thing to lie nearly asleep in the loft and have rain pattering across the roof. He had always thought of it as the river coming back, to renew itself and begin again.

Here, it was something else, a wet and miserable fact of nature that he had not even considered in his efforts to survive. And why? He had lived among concealing mountains all his life and knew very well the suddenness with which the weather could change. Only now, when it was dark and too late to do anything about it, did he see the necessity of making his nights more secure against the elements.

Lying in a shallow trench covered with needles was fine for keeping warm and, as long as the rain did not last, he would even stay reasonably dry. But if it did last, the water would eventually soak through to leave him wet, cold, and sleepless for the rest of the night. If it started coming fast enough, the run-off that filled the gullies and ravines would also seep in around him until he was lying in three or four inches of water.

No great amounts of wisdom were needed to see that a small ditch scratched into the ground on the uphill side would eliminate the danger of water running into his bed. And although he lacked tools and was limited to materials at hand, it was easy to see how his bed could be sheltered against the rain.

The structure he had in mind was simply a pair of forked uprights holding a cross-piece. Leaning across the latter from both sides, making it look something like a tent, were two thick walls of heavily-needled pine boughs. That was all there was to it.

Chris did not suppose it would be absolutely rainproof. However, he was sure that such a thing over his bed would spell the difference between a reasonable night and a bad one.

The idea of stopping earlier, to have time and light enough to build the shelter, was not a pleasing one; a mile might be walked in that time. But then, common horse-sense said he would not get home at all if he came down with pneumonia.

It could only be hoped that luck would be with him, this time. For now, at least, the rain was little more than a shower. Still, it rankled him to be caught like that. And his disgust, coming in concert with random and worrisome drops of rain that splashed in his face, kept sleep at a distance.

Not until an hour or so later when the dripping stopped—and it was odd that it stopped because Chris could still hear rain falling beyond the tree—was he able to drift off for a while.

The boy came awake again, hard, still hearing from somewhere in his sleep a sound that was like heaven splitting open. He did not know what it was; whether it had been real or only dreamed.

But there was a strangeness about, and the forest was full of furtive sounds. Chris strained his ears, trying to identify them, and was puzzled. They were not the noises animals made. On a night like this, the creatures would tuck themselves deep into burrow and den and sleep until it passed. This was something else, just beneath the sound of rain.

It was more like groaning, a crying, and it came faintly from every direction. The boy still could not tell what was doing it, and his scalp began to crawl.

Then, with an abruptness that made him sit bolt upright, a sharp crack as loud as his father's rifle filled the air, and a heavy limb crashed to the ground only a few yards away!

Chris jumped up and pressed against the tree. Whimpering, Griper soon joined him and they huddled there, each perhaps as frightened as the other. But at least what was happening was no longer a mystery.

Rain was clinging to branches and needles, and turning to ice. Those peculiar sounds were limbs crying under the growing weight of it; when the burden became too great, they snapped and tore loose.

Chris knew he and Griper had to get away from the trees, quickly. Falling limbs were killers, and the danger increased with every drop of rain that

fell. Along the river was best. They would have more open sky above them there.

The boy hesitated for a moment longer, wishing he could see. It was a bad time for moving around. Other than a feeble, almost indiscernible gray above the trees, darkness was complete. But there was no alternative.

Swinging his spear from side to side in front of him, and with the uncertainty of one who has been blindfolded, Chris began making his way down through the forest.

He did not have to worry about losing his direction and wandering in circles; both the sloping ground and the sound of the river were there to guide him. The problem was in moving from one point to the next, and he wished he could see the dog to follow him.

Little things that one did not notice or think about in the light of day, became unforeseen and treacherous obstacles in the dark. The forest floor was littered with the windfall of age and countless storms. There were fallen trees and rotting limbs to get past. Rocks jutted up, and the ground itself was far from being even. Where pine, spruce, or cedar gave way to hardwoods like maple and aspen, bushes grew in tangled profusion.

It was an agonizing, one step at a time proposition. For every minute spent going forward, it seemed, ten were spent backing away and going round. How many times he tripped, fell, or scraped painfully against something, Chris did not know.

And through all of it was the knowledge that, somewhere above him, an ice-laden limb might be just seconds away from breaking and hurtling down. Those shot-like reports were coming more often now, from every direction.

The familiar forest had become cavernous and alien, a labyrinth to be threaded in the midst of eerie conflict. The heavens marched there with ice, and a rooted, unmoving army protested and fought to endure. A nightmare could not have been more frightening or seemingly so far removed from reality.

In his blindness the boy could not at any time tell how much progress he had made, or how far he had yet to go. It was not until the rain fell harder across his face, and the river's voice was suddenly no longer muffled by the forest, that Chris realized he had finally made it.

From then on, there was nothing left for them to do but keep to the river's edge and walk until that freezing night was over.

It was a bleak and disheartening thing to contemplate. He was already soaked through and shaking badly in that wintry downpour; Griper was miserable too, he was sure. Except when it was part of some game, like deviling the ducks in the marsh, the black Labrador did not like being wet. But how much of the night remained before them could only be guessed. Whether measured in minutes or hours, it would still seem an eternity.

Chris picked his way along the river shore,

having only the dim and phantom sky above to guide him, and gloomily considered his lot. With every drop of rain telling him how cold he was, and how much colder he would be, it was hard to think beyond this night and conceive of anything being worse. And yet, the hard and bitter truth was that trouble had only just begun.

Morning was coming, of course, no matter how far away it seemed, and he looked forward to it with a great longing. The temperature would rise, and they could stop to rest with the one consolation of being farther along in the journey. The skies might clear by then and bring the blessing of sunshine. But the fact was that it did not really make much difference whether the rain stopped or not . . . not in terms of tomorrow night, the night after that or, indeed, for a long time to come.

In the warming air of morning, the ice that was forming would begin to thaw and give the forest a rainstorm of its own. The ground-covering needles that provided warm beds, comparatively dry even now because of the freezing, would be soaked through and useless.

Griper had some protection in his coat and, like all dogs, was less bothered by cold, anyway. But Chris saw himself, from there on, having to sleep during the daylight hours and to travel at night. If it had to be, then it had to be. He would do whatever was necessary to get home; there had never been any question of that.

Surely, he thought, there were other ways of

staying warm! He could not have exhausted all the possibilities. If only he had some way of killing a bear . . . the skin would be as big and warm as the one on the floor by his parents' bed. If only, he thought, he could discover the secret of starting a fire. If only . . .

The boy hunched against the rain and groaned with the futility he felt. It was easy enough, he told himself, to fling wishes around as he went. But, for all the hope there was of seeing them come true, he might as well have wished that these days and nights had never happened.

Chapter Twelve

Dawn was lost that morning and never came. The hour of sunrise was nearly at hand before the darkness below the clouds began to dissolve into milky gray and the river could be seen again.

It found Christian Holm huddled against Griper beneath the sheltering overhang of a house-sized boulder. Almost frozen, he was neither awake nor really asleep.

Not until the boy felt the warming air did he stir and sit up, and blink in bewilderment at his surroundings. He could not recall coming there. Chris knew that he had not planned to stop and, remembering the blackness and rain, could not even imagine his being able to find such a place. He supposed Griper had led him there.

The rain had stopped, and the icy sting was

gone from the air, and Chris was tempted to curl up and stay. He was tired. But there were things to be done. A fish had to be speared, new shoes were needed, and something had to be done about the coming night. It was not enough to curl up with the dog. He supposed he could bury himself in the sand beneath another sheltering rock. The sand was rather damp and clammy, though, perhaps being too close to underground seepage from the river, and he wanted to look around and see if he could not do better.

Too, there were indications of a clearing six or seven hundred feet above the river. He wanted to make the climb as soon as he tended to the fish and shoes. Common sense and those low-hanging clouds nagged at him not to waste himself like that. But he would not listen. The boy ignored these things and—denying what he knew was the real reason for going—argued that climbing to study the lay of the land was something that simply had to be done now and again.

Chris found shallows a short distance upstream, and settled down on a rock to wait. He supposed it was not a very good day for fishing. There was no sun to warm the water, and the few flying insects that had survived the frosts must have, he thought, perished during the night.

It took more than an hour, and his patience was sorely tried; time was too important. But, at last, a fish did appear. It came into the shallows, swimming ever so slowly. As if heavy with the dullness of that day, it rested for long minutes on the bottom before answering to the whispers of some furtive little current and rising again. Twice, it headed for the rock and then slipped away to swim just out of reach. His spirits low, and close to giving up, Chris crouched there for half of another hour before the chance finally came.

"Come on! Come on," he whispered to the fish. "Just a little closer."

Chris jabbed hard and fast, and grunted with satisfaction when he felt the weight jumping on the end of his spear.

The boy clambered back with his prize and, after feeding Griper, sat down for the first time to eat without hesitation.

Morning was only an hour older when, shod in stiff new shoes of bark, Chris started the climb to the clearing. Griper continued upstream and then stopped to look back, questioningly.

"This way, boy! Come on," he called, and the Labrador returned to follow reluctantly at his heels.

He had picked the worst part of that day for climbing. Although the danger from breaking limbs had passed, the water from melted ice was still raining down; he was cold and wet again before going very far. But hours would pass before it stopped, and he had to make the climb now. It could not wait.

Chris paused in the shadowed timber once, to

catch his breath, and went on. No, it could not wait, and there was no longer any pretense about it. He still tried not to think about what might be seen from the clearing. It could not be allowed to have importance beforehand, lest disappointment come full and scalding. But the notion that the mountains of home *might* now be in sight would not let him alone. And, as was inevitable, hope rose like a fever with every step he took.

When the trees began to thin and the clearing opened up before him, Chris ran the rest of the way and stood, gasping for breath, searching the north.

Oceans of gray, drifting clouds were there, and nothing more. Clouds, and the slopes of unfamiliar mountains lifting into the mists no more than four or five miles distant.

"If it was clear," he told Griper, "the saddle would be there. It has to be! We just can't see it now, that's all. Just can't see . . ."

Chris sighed, knowing he was only trying to fool himself into feeling better. Of course the mountain *might* be near. There was no proof to the contrary. But it could just as easily not be there, and flinging hopes or threats at the clouds would not change things in the slightest. He still had to go on with the effort to stay alive.

With Griper following and then running ahead, the boy began retracing his steps down through the forest. Perhaps it was better, he thought, not to

118

know than to look at the far curve of the horizon and see no end to his journey.

When he reached the river again, Chris settled down to walking, as he had been doing, it seemed, since time began. Where was he? Where had he got to? The river had taken him far from the life he had known and now ignored his puny efforts to return. And yet, except for the dog, in all that wild country the river was the one familiar thing left to him—a voice he had heard all his life, a face he knew, a compass, and the one thread that was still tied to home.

Chris speared another fish early in the afternoon. He gave Griper the head and tail to quiet him and, saving the rest for evening, went on. As he walked, he studied the world around him, looking for another way of staying warm at night.

It was in the middle of this thus far unrewarded search that something else crept into his awareness. Chris found himself stopping and turning around to watch the shadows in the forest. Griper was not acting up in any way, and yet he had a distinct feeling, like a finger on his spine, that they were not alone.

But he neither saw nor heard anything; the forest was quiet and still. Not a single bird fluttered in its depths to give it life, and the only sound was that of the river.

Chris took a deep breath and, attributing the feeling to his imagination, resumed walking. This day, its clouds and missing sun, did press down on mind and spirit with gloom and trepidation.

He was grateful for Griper's presence. But the dog could not give him the remembered brightness of home and human companionship, the laughter of love, and—he thought of it almost fondly—even the warmth of angry scolding. In a way, then, he had been alone and lost too long in heavy, river-filled silences. And there was nothing left inside with which to resist such an assault.

Chris turned and led the way across the sand to massive, water-carved boulders and sat down. He was close to crying, and he felt cold.

It was not the kind of cold that pushes mercury down into the bulb of a thermometer or turns breath to fog. He merely needed comfort and reassurance, something to put between him and that deadly day and to push back the dark when it came. And what was there? He had neither lamp nor wall, nor hearth and soft braided rug. There was nothing.

If only, he thought, he could have a fire. With a crackling blaze, none of this would matter as much. It would drive the grayness from his bones, cook his food, and on the coldest, darkest of nights he would be warm and not quite as lost. . . .

Chris stood up and looked toward the trees, halfway expecting to see someone or something moving there. Again it appeared vacant and devoid of life.

He sat down again, still thinking about a fire.

But how could he even hope to start one? Certainly, his first attempt had been less than promising.

The principle of it, Chris knew, was simple. Two pieces of wood rubbed together created heat by means of friction. When the heat reached a certain point, combustion took place.

Pawing through a scattering of driftwood left under and around the boulders by high water, he found a couple of dry, bone-like remnants of a branch and, looking at them, tried to figure out what he had been doing wrong. Griper watched with interest for a moment, but then settled down to rest.

Chris braced one and rubbed hard and fast with the other. As before, the wood grew hot to the touch, and no more than that. The air seemed to be cooling it off as fast as he could generate the heat. Aggravated by failure and by his tiring hands, the boy went through the motions slowly, and realized that the rubbing-stick was not passing across the other in exactly the same place each time. The air *was* cooling it then! But how in the world was he going to keep that from happening and rub fast enough, all at the same time?

The fire-bow that he remembered apparently eliminated that problem. It was not the same, of course; one piece of wood turned, rather than sawed, against the other. A round spindle whirled rapidly against a flat piece of wood . . . and there

121

was only one thing that would keep it from dancing and skittering around like a top. A hole!

Pleased with his discovery, Chris almost
grinned. The hole kept the friction in one place,
and also protected it from the cooling air.

But a fire-bow was still out of the question.
Without a piece of heavy cording or a leather
thong, he simply had no way of making one. Chris
remembered ruefully that his new boots—had he
gotten them—would have long, leather laces. And
he wished that he had gone to look for the wreck-
age of the raft. The rope holding the logs together,
unraveled into its separate strands, could have been
used.

There was always the material in his clothes,
and the idea of cutting a strip and twisting it into
a bowstring did occur. But he was neither sure that
it would be durable enough, nor that it would grip
the spindle properly. It did not seem worth the
gamble.

Thinking about it, though, had taught him a
thing or two. Friction was the important part,
friction and some way of controlling it.

With two sticks, a hole would not work. The
boy decided he needed a notch in one . . . and
some way of holding the other with both hands to
avoid tiring so quickly.

He examined the pieces of wood, perplexed by
the problem. A notch was easy enough, but if he
used both hands on one stick, what would keep the
other from jumping around?

It was enough to make him throw the pieces down in disgust. Own up to it, he told himself. You don't know how and you're just wasting time!

But Chris did not get up. He sat there for a while, hunched over and staring at nothing. That gray and hopeless day stood before him, an insurmountable wall, and would not let him move; nagged into it, he finally picked up the wood again. If nothing else, the problem kept his mind away from other things.

All right, he thought, use your head. One piece has to be braced some way. Maybe if it were bigger . . . yes, he decided, if one were big enough to brace with his feet or sit on . . . if it could be straddled and gripped with the knees, it would hold still. On the other hand, the notch would be sideways to him then, and he guessed it would be too awkward. The only way to avoid it was to have the notch run the length of the wood. But . . . well, why not a groove? It accomplished the same thing, did it not? Indeed, he thought, it might even be better, particularly if the rubbing stick were shaped to fit as snugly as the spindle did its hole.

Chris, seeing hope in his reasoning, roused Griper and hurried along the river to find what he needed. Driftwood, whether big or small, was not in short supply. The only requirement, other than size, was that it be dry. He quickly found a shattered limb nearly as big as himself. It rested, half-buried, just inside the entrance to a cave-like place formed by a tremendous slab of rock leaning across its neighbor.

Leaving the limb where it was, braced nicely by the sand, Chris took his knife and went to work. The prospects of this place excited him. Griper had already expressed approval by snuggling against a wall and dropping once more into sleep. Gathered here were all the potentials of a pleasant and comfortable night. Soft sand, fish to eat, plenty of wood, and a better shelter than any he could have built himself. All it needed was the magic touch of fire.

He made a V-shaped groove, just a few inches long, and saved the shavings from it. The rubbing-stick was next. Chris painstakingly whittled one end down to the right size and shape. When that was done, he was ready to try.

It was not without a certain amount of misgiving that Chris placed the tool in the groove and, bearing down with both hands, began pushing it back and forth. Like some inventor coming to the moment of testing and truth, he was afraid of having indulged in foolish dreams.

He worked hard for a full five minutes and nothing came of it—nothing that he could see. Tired, out of breath, and certain that failure was dogging him again, Chris stopped to touch the groove. But it was hot enough to make him yank his finger away. Stung and surprised, he began again, working the tool with new energy.

Another five minutes passed, ten, and then

fifteen. His arms were ready to fall off, and the groove was doing nothing except turn in color from near-white to dark yellow. Patience wavered in the face of it, threatening to die, and he had constantly to remind himself that he had never seen it done and, therefore, could not possibly know what to expect.

Patience, yes, he had to have that.

The minutes slipped by, and that shelter of stone, for all its promise, held only the heaviness of his breathing. He watched the wood change merely from yellow to brown, and despaired in it because it was not enough and his strength was nearly gone.

Chris sensed defeat; the sour-faced shadow of it was already there, waiting to be acknowledged. But he could not accept it gracefully. Losing his temper, he attacked the groove with a spiteful burst of speed. And in anger came the first, curling wisp of smoke.

A tiny spot of red, no bigger than a spark, glowed in the middle of the groove. It took the boy a moment to gain control of his amazement and do what had to be done.

Blowing on it ever so gently, Chris touched the smallest and finest shavings to the ember, and the glowing began to spread. Quickly he added more shavings and splinters, watching the smoke increase. The smell of it was heaven. Finally he blew a little harder, and the bits of wood burst into flame.

With his heart pounding in his throat, he carefully fed the infant's hunger, progressing from splinters to twigs, twigs to finger-sized fragments of branches, and finally the heavier chunks that would burn more slowly and last for a while.

It was not, however, until after he had gathered several armloads of wood along the river shore and stacked them outside the shelter that Chris allowed himself to sit back and enjoy his triumph. And triumph it was, even though Griper merely sighed and looked at him, as if to ask why it had not been done before.

Equipped with little more than his wits, he had slept warm at night, fashioned a spear, fed himself, made shoes of a sort, and now had evoked the miracle of fire! Chris grinned broadly and reveled in its cheery brightness.

Only Heaven knew how far he had yet to travel, and if he would ever see home again. The miles were long and arduous, and the perils were quite real. His confrontation with the big Cinnamon, the near breaking of his ankle, and last night's freezing rain were proof of it.

But, for now at least, none of it could have mattered less or seemed more remote.

Chapter Thirteen

The fire was dead. So it seemed, at least, when the cold first pushed him from sleep. Darkness filled the shelter; its walls no longer danced to the flickering of flames, and for one startled moment Chris could almost accuse himself of having dreamed the whole thing.

But the cold was not the cold that pierced the night outside, the smell of smoke was still in the air, and as he came more clearly awake the boy saw that a few coals still glowed dimly in the ashes.

Chris heaved a sigh and sat up. It was all right. There was still time to rake the coals together and add some light wood. The fire would soon leap back into merry life.

It had been his intention to get up every few

hours to put on more wood. He had merely underestimated his weariness and the luxury of that place. Too, the wood had been curing in the sand and sun, perhaps for years. Even the heaviest chunks burned fast and much like kindling, leaving little in the way of enduring embers.

After this, he sleepily told himself, some of his wood supply would come from the forest.

The silence in there struck him, then. He had gone to sleep with Griper's contented snoring to remind him that he was not alone. Now it had stopped, and, reaching out for him, Chris found that the dog had left. The discovery worried him.

But he supposed Griper, like any other dog, might have become restless and wanted to nose around outside for a while. There was also some cooked fish left—the boy had grown too sleepy to finish it—and he knew that Griper, tormented by its smell, could have gone hunting on his own. Whatever the case, the retriever was sure to be back before long.

Yawning and shivering a little, Chris started to go get some of the wood stacked outside. He had no more than raised up on his knees, though, when he suddenly became aware that there was something moving around just beyond the entrance.

He knew by its cautious behavior that it was not Griper, and at first he thought a raccoon or fox had come, attracted by the smell of fish. Those thieving creatures grew bold when it was quiet and fires had flickered out. But he heard, faintly, the sound of it walking back and forth out there—its breathing slow and deep—and knew that it was much bigger! A bear, gray timber wolf . . . what? He pressed hard against a wall of his shelter, frightened and wishing he could see.

It brought forcibly to mind that feeling of being followed the day before . . . the strangeness in the air that had twice made him stop to question the forest and its shadows. Maybe it was coincidence, but Chris wondered now if it had been this creature and not his imagination after all.

He wanted to yell and throw something, in hopes of driving the intruder away, until he remembered the bobcat's lack of fear. This animal, whatever it was, had no reason to fear humans and might only be antagonized by that kind of behavior.

But the boy knew he might be in danger and was too scared to stand and do nothing. What if the animal decided to come in? For a moment Chris considered his spear. The sharp points might drive it off. On the other hand, like a bee sting, the flimsy weapon might only make matters worse.

Everything depended on what his visitor wanted, whether it was prowling around out of curiosity or hunger, and if it was the latter, whether it wanted him, the fish, or both. Chris, not wanting to wait and find out, decided to play it safe by retreating.

He crawled out the other end of the shelter and,

not daring to run for a tree, felt for holds on the boulder's surface and frantically began to climb. Neither a bear nor a wolf, if the creature were one of the two, would be able to follow.

When he reached the top, some fifteen feet above the sand, Chris inched his way forward on hands and knees until he came to the edge. There were no stars, no wisping light of moon; he could not see any more there than he had from his shelter. He could only listen and perhaps puzzle out the animal's identity.

For a long time he heard nothing, and he wondered if the intruder had gone. Certainly, while he was climbing, it would have had ample opportunity to sneak in, grab the fish, and leave. It was possible, too, that his abrupt departure had alarmed it. In this darkness the animal was as blind as he was, and, detecting an unfamiliar scent, could not have known the nature of the creature inside the shelter. Unless, of course, it had followed him the day before.

With the return of that eerie thought he also realized that, out there in the open, the river was louder. The vague sounds he had heard before— the breathing, curiously remembered now as being more like hissing, and the ever so slight disturbance of padded feet pressing into sand littered with willow leaves, twigs, and pebbles—would be lost in the rushing of water, even though the river was quieter here than in most places.

Not knowing where the animal might be, Chris

gave up any notion of returning to the shelter. For now it was safer to stay where he was.

He sat down on the rock to shiver and wait, wondering if Griper was not caught in the same predicament somewhere nearby. Poor dog, he thought. That Labrador was always more bluff than bite. Sometimes he challenged the big animals, sometimes he did not. Either way, Griper was easily intimidated by them.

The muffled snap of breaking wood reached his ears and made him jump. It came from below, inside the shelter. Chris held his breath. The beast was not only still around, it had found the fish and, in the act of stealing it, had broken his spear!

There was nothing more after that. The night and the river closed about him with seeming emptiness. But as before, the silence could not be trusted and he did not change his mind about staying atop the boulder. Angry about having to spend valuable time making another spear in the morning, Chris flailed his arms back and forth across his chest in an effort to keep from freezing.

He could only hope that the darkness was nearly over.

Chapter Fourteen

The heavy, somber clouds were still there. That hour of morning which, on promising days, came as if seen through the smoked glass of a lamp chimney, was confined to the hidden sky somewhere above the forested rim of the world. Dawn was lost to him again, and a light drizzle had begun to fall. Chris huddled against it, watching the slow emergence of river and sand in the failing gloom.

Below, the ashes of his fire would be cold and truly dead; his spear was broken, and the meat he had saved for breakfast was gone. Although another spear could be made and the secret of fire was still his, he could not help feeling that, so soon after forgiving his trespass, nature had turned against him once more.

After a careful study of the river shore and the darker edge of the forest, Chris decided it was safe to leave. His visitor was not to be seen. Neither was Griper, for that matter, and he had to be found. Making his way to the rear of the rock, and seeing where he had come during the night, the boy prudently tried to work some of the stiffness from his muscles. Again, he had climbed where, in the absence of danger, climbing would have seemed impossible.

It was when, three or four minutes later, he got down on his stomach and felt with his toes for a narrow ledge that he sensed something moving in the forest. Holding still, Chris waited for it to happen again, and then saw not last night's predator but a magnificently antlered elk coming down through the trees toward the river.

As many times as he had seen them near the edge of the clearing at home, Chris still found himself watching with fascination. He remained where he was, not wanting to scare the elegant animal away before it had a chance to drink.

The elk bore scars from many battles and seemed quite old. Probably it had come to that inevitable time when the challenges of younger bulls could no longer be met, and now lived the lonely life of an outcast.

No more than fifty feet away, it came into a space of open ground close to the river and the forest's edge. There, the elk stopped abruptly to test the air; its ears nervously turned this way and that to examine the silences beneath the rushing of water.

For a moment Chris thought the animal had become aware of his presence. The wind was wrong though, and he had not made even the slightest noise. It was something else, there in the misted dark of surrounding trees. The elk watched and listened in the rain, and suddenly wheeled in an attempt to regain the depths of the forest. But it was too late. Turning, the elk stopped and held still, and Chris saw its enemy moving in a silent, muscular crouch away from the shadows and into the open. He knew now what had followed them the day before, and what had come prowling when the fire was dead . . . a *mountain lion!*

A chill deeper than the cold of that wet morning passed through Chris. He remembered it being said around Bodwin's Landing that the big cats were shy creatures. Of course, a female with young was best left alone, and a cornered lion would fight with unbelievable fury. But, these exceptions aside, the lions were not considered dangerous and were a problem only in that they sometimes molested livestock.

Knowing this was of no comfort to the boy. Seeing the lion coming, its yellow eyes full of death, it was hard to think in terms of shyness. Where was the proof that the rules always applied? Whether out of curiosity or hunger, the cat *had* followed. . . .

With a harsh scream the lion ended its stalking

135

and came exploding across that open ground. For one frightening second the elk did not move. It stood as if already overwhelmed and without hope. It was not until the last instant, when the cat was ready to leap, that the elk lowered its antlers and braced itself for the impact. Spitting violently, and barely avoiding that bristling barrier, the lion retreated. It circled slowly to look for a weakness in the other's defenses.

Pressing down hard against the boulder to make himself small, Chris waited for the next move in that deadly game. He had no doubt about the outcome. The lion was young and in its prime, while the elk, weary and perhaps with dimming vision, had come to its final years. It was a sad affair, and in another time and place he could have wished that the old warrior might somehow win. But there was no room for sentiment here; Chris had himself to think about. He wanted the lion to win and eat its fill, so that it would go somewhere and sleep. It was the only way he could be sure of resuming his journey without fear of that devil haunting his steps.

Chris held his breath as the tawny cat began to run in that tight circle. The elk, pivoting on its long legs, was hard put to keep facing its enemy. And there seemed to be no end to it. The turning went on and on into dizzying monotony, fast, slow, fast again until . . .

So quickly did the lion reverse direction and launch itself across the circle that Chris nearly

cried out. The elk was caught off stride and faltered, and in that brief moment the lion gained its back. Riding its staggering victim halfway to the ground, with claws cutting deep, the cat fought for the throat and the one, swift bite that would end it all.

But then the elk reared up and, raking desperately with its antlers, managed to scrape its tormentor loose and break free. Before the sprawling cat could recover, the elk rose stiff-legged and came down with its sharp hooves. Catching the thrust hard in the ribs, the lion shrieked with pain and scrambled out of reach.

Chris watched with amazement as that powerful beast retreated to a safe distance. Perplexed, the cat stared at the elk and hesitantly went back to circling.

In all that wilderness the mountain lion had no equal. It was prey to no other animal, matched in strength only by the bear, and without peer in speed and cunning. And yet this old bull had taken the full brunt of the attack and still stood, defiantly holding its ground.

Chris tried to be patient. Next time, he told himself. The elk was hurt and bleeding, and surely could not keep up its admirable defense much longer. Soon the lion would have its way and he could leave.

The big cat moved slowly at first, as if thinking and sizing up its quarry anew. But, like a quiet wind growing, the pace quickened and the circling became the same lethal thing that it was before. Several times during the next hour the lion spun in its tracks and hurtled, screaming, toward the center. And each time the antlers were there to turn the attack aside.

After that the cat appeared to be less certain of its quarry. Purpose seemed gone from its turning. It walked and ran, and made a few half-hearted attempts to reach the elk. Mostly the lion walked, and it had begun to punctuate its steps with growling and a deep-throated moaning. To Chris it sounded very much like an overgrown house-cat complaining about a mouse it could not catch. For a long interval the animal even sat down to pant and watch the river through the trees.

Puzzled by the change, Chris waited to see what would come of it. Maybe, the boy thought, it was more of the lion's cunning ways, a ruse to throw the elk off guard. But if it was just a trick, it was a little too convincing to suit him. The cat *did* look tired and thirsty. Anxiously Chris wondered if he had made a bad mistake in not leaving earlier. . .

Hopefully studying the elk, he looked for some sign that the old fellow might be growing complacent—anything that would spur the lion into attacking with renewed fury—and there was nothing. Whether the cat walked, stood, or broke into a slow run, the elk remained alert and ready. Not until the lion stopped and slumped down for a third time did the elk appear to relax its vigil. It snuffed at the ground, raised up to gaze at the forest, and unconcernedly turned to lick its wounds. Then it looked back at the lion and suddenly *charged!*

Caught by surprise, and hesitating as if it did not believe what it saw, the lion had time only to scramble ignominiously into the trees. Instead of pressing the attack, however, the elk returned to the center of the clearing and waited.

Chris stared dumbfounded at the spot where the lion had disappeared. One minute went slowly by, and another, and still nothing moved there. Where had the big cat gone? Had it given up to go wandering off in the forest, or was it merely waiting somewhere close in that covering green?

The elk was staying put. Its ears constantly probed beyond the edge of the clearing, and Chris knew this might be an indication that the lion was still around. Unfortunately it could just as easily be nothing more than caution. The elk would be understandably reluctant to leave that open ground until absolutely certain the danger has passed.

Chris shuddered, cold and wet, and wondered what to do. He wanted to climb down, find Griper, and be on his way. And maybe it would be all right. Maybe the lion was coming back, and maybe it would win. *Maybe*— He closed his eyes and stifled a groan. There was no certainty in any of it, no guarantee that once he left the safety of the boulder the lion would not be on his trail within a mile. Perhaps it had followed out of curiosity before, but who could say that, frustrated and angry, it would not be looking for an easier mark now.

He heard something—a small sound almost lost in the dim patter of rain—and jerked his eyes open. It was only the elk turning around and pawing at the soft earth. He supposed the old bull was cold and impatient too.

Slowly the boy shifted his position and tried to get comfortable. Chris felt as if he had been there forever. He was just a few feet above the place where, only hours ago, there had been a warm fire and Griper's reassuring presence, and yet these things already seemed remote in his memory.

The elk snorted, and Chris looked again, and saw the lion standing at the edge of the trees. It had come back!

He realized that, instead of leaving or merely resting, the cat had been slowly inching around the clearing to get behind the bull. But either sound or scent had betrayed the effort, and the elk was first to move. Having driven the lion out of the clearing once, it rushed forward in an attempt to do it again.

The lion was ready this time, and sprang lightly aside. In danger of being cut off from center ground, the elk stopped short and quickly moved back. With that, the game began again. The cat returned to the tactic of running, and the circle was smaller than before and harder to follow.

Now, Chris told himself. *Get away from here!*

The lion might win, and maybe the fight would

come to nothing, but he could not stay to find out. He put his weight on the ledge, found a handhold, and eased downward. When the ledge was at eye level, he carefully shifted his grip and held on to it. His muscles trembling with the strain, the boy searched the boulder's face for the next place to put his feet. There was a crack below him, a fissure, and stretching down to hang at arms' length Chris located it with his toes. But when he tried to move one hand, the other slipped on the wet surface of the ledge and he fell. Luckily it was for no more than five or six feet, and he landed in soft sand. Suffering nothing worse than a skinned elbow, Chris hurried into the shelter, grabbed his shoes, and rushed out again to run hard along the river's edge.

Gradually the cat's sharp and angry screams began to fade. When he had gone perhaps half a mile, Chris stopped to put his shoes on and catch his breath, and there, sitting under a tree and growling at the distant sounds, was Griper.

Chris whistled and the dog came to him, almost crawling, to press against his legs.

"Come on, boy," he tugged the retriever's ears. "Let's get away from here."

The rain, forgotten in the excitement, still fell in a slow drizzle; night's coldness persisted in that gray, morning air.

It was not until around noon that they stopped again. Chris was no longer concerned about the lion; there was safety in distance. Wet, miserable, and seeing a likely place, he had finally permitted himself to think about a fire.

The shelter was just a hollow in the side of a single boulder, and not nearly as nice as the last one. But it did not matter. There were still good miles left in the day, and a fish to catch. He wanted only to drive the chill from his bones, make another spear, and nap for a while.

The dog waited out of the rain while he went to look for wood. Dry fuel was scarce now. It took several minutes of searching before, in a jam of logs and stone, he found a heavy chunk that had not been soaked by the rain. Dragging it to the shelter and bracing it in the sand, Chris went out again and came back with an armload of twigs and small branches.

The boy knew, almost before he reached in his pocket for it, that the knife was gone. His fingers had not yet touched the bottom seam when his heart skipped a beat and he remembered putting it aside in the other shelter, putting it down in his anxious efforts to build a fire, and *not picking it up again!*

Chris sat there, stunned for a moment, and then grabbed a piece of wood to slam it against the wall of stone. Why? How could he have done such a thing! Breaking into tears, he stumbled out into the rain to go on walking. He could not, dared not, go back.

What, he wondered, was the use? How could anything matter now?

And in that desperate moment, he saw the first dancing, fluttering flake of snow.

Chapter Fifteen

Chris sucked his breath in sharply and stopped. Wiping the tears from his eyes, he tensely watched the sky and the contrasting dark of the forest to his right. Telling himself that it did not necessarily mean anything, he tried not to be alarmed; one flake did not make a blizzard, and it was quite common to have a few harmless flurries come salting across the mountains days before the season of snows began in earnest.

But he was like a child who, having a nightmare, wanted to wake and find better dreams. Even as he watched, the soft drapery of rain began to change. A second flake traced its way down across the forest's darkness, and three more, and then they came too quickly to be counted. The truth could no longer be put aside.

All his days of walking had been a race against this moment, and he had lost. Chris wondered if, indeed, the race had not been lost from the very start. Long before raft and river carried him deep into limbo, there had been warnings in the cold fire of autumn leaves. The big Canadian geese were high-flying and arrow-swift prophets when they left lake and marsh to look for warmer days. Yes, and the almost imperceptible way the air had seemed to brighten, the sudden closeness of far mountains, and the sweet tang of woodsmoke . . . all those less obvious things were foretokens of this event.

The only question had been how soon, how quickly would it come? And now he knew the answer. Chris hurried back to the shelter and huddled there to watch.

Just as rain could stop abruptly, so could snow. But seeing the sky and the clouded ridges slowly drift from sight until only the nearer trees and a remnant of river were left, Chris saw no hope of such a thing; the ground was already turning white.

It had to be decided, now, whether it was best to stay where he was, to go on walking for as long as he could, or perhaps try to make it back to where he had left the knife.

Lion or no, the latter was still out of the question. It would be dark before he could get there, and in this snow the chances of walking right past it were that much greater.

In fact, looking at his loss in the glum aftermath

of surprise, and considering what was happening now, he was not sure the knife was that important. Of course, it would enable him to make another spear, but to what end? Who, in falling snow, could see well enough to aim? And afterward? Chris did not remember ever seeing fish once the snow had come. He supposed they retreated to deeper pools and waited under the thickening ice until the thaw.

Too, the knife had helped him start a fire. But again, looking at it more carefully, the boy had to admit that the knife might have been more of a convenience than a necessity. While it would take more time and effort, he guessed a rubbing stick would work without being so carefully shaped. A groove could be made with a sharp stone.

Having reached this conclusion, and terribly conscious of being wet and cold, Chris decided to stay and try to build a fire. It would be good to follow Griper's example and rest for a while. Past winters had taught him how tiring it was to walk with just a few inches of snow on the ground. He picked up a likely-looking stone, but then hesitated, realizing the situation was even worse than he had thought.

What was he going to eat, and *when?* It was not just a matter of being unable to fish. The storm might end that night or in the morning; it could also last for days. But even now the snow was covering and killing the greens that had helped sustain him. The enduring onions would be impossible to find. The appalling fact was that from now on both he and Griper were going to be entirely without food!

Chris looked at the stone he held, and let it drop. From the very beginning, time had been precious. With the first falling flake, its importance had become incredible. And in the face of it, however desirable, the value of a fire was questionable. A fire took time to build, and time to accomplish its purpose. What was the use? Five minutes after leaving one, he would be as cold as ever and, if snow still fell, just as wet.

Where, then, was there a choice? Without food and faced with long miles of cold and deepening snow, he knew time was against him. The only thing he could do was walk for as long as strength lasted. After that . . .

"I'm sorry, boy. We've got to go. Come on."

Uncertain and frightened, he left the shelter and moved on. With tail tucked between his legs, the dog fell into step ahead of him. Chris tried not to think. For whatever time the spirit might endure, nothing else could be allowed to matter. One foot in front of the other, over and over again; that was how it had to be.

As they walked, the snowfall slowly increased in volume until Chris could see no more than an arm's length ahead. Griper was a dark ghost in that whiteness, seen and then not seen. Only his tracks remained constant.

With the sound of the river to guide them, it was

impossible to lose direction. But going through that thickly swirling and endless wall, the boy had the feeling he was forever stepping to the edge of a precipice. The last of solid earth was beneath his feet; empty and yawning space had to lie just beyond.

He tried to ignore the sensation and walk a little faster. Distance had to be covered, and time made to count. Time . . . as if frozen and made to stand still by infinite white, it seemed not to pass at all. They walked, but where was the proof that they moved, that they were not locked in that space where one minute had died and the next had yet to begin? And still, time's vague signature was there; he became increasingly aware of it gathering beneath his feet.

Chris stopped to kneel down and, to his dismay, found that the snow was already three or four inches deep. But the dog whimpered at him and they went on.

It could not keep up like that, he thought. It *had* to stop!

Many times during the rest of the afternoon Chris tried to convince himself that it was slowing down. But the deception never worked. By the time evening came, the snow was halfway to his knees.

Thus far, the cold had not seemed as bad as anticipated. He could thank the heavy exertions of walking for that, and very probably the temperature was not as low as it had been on some of those brilliant nights earlier in his journey. In the last hour or two, though, his feet had begun to trouble him; there was not much feeling left in them.

Chris decided he had better stop and try to do something about it. The bark-shoes helped, of course, and maybe there was not too much to worry about as long as he kept moving. But later, it would be colder and dark, and he knew it was best not to take chances.

Whistling for Griper, the boy turned and picked his way through the trees. As could be expected, the snow was not as deep in the forest. He saw mounds here and there where limbs had bent to lose the burden of it, but much of the snow had yet to reach the ground. Walking was easier; if it had not been for the greater number of obstacles, and the danger of breaking limbs, Chris would have taken advantage of it.

It was one of those obstacles that he was looking for; casualties of age and winds, and part of that ever-turning cycle of birth and death, they were common in the forest. Coming to a dead giant that had fallen across the trunk of another, he looked underneath and found that it met his needs.

Free of snow, because there had not been a wind to make it drift, the underside of the tree provided a place for him to sit down and work on his feet away from the weather. Crawling in, Chris discovered that he could even sit upright without bumping his head. Griper joined him, shaking the snow from his coat and wagging his tail.

In that instant of stopping, he realized how close he was to exhaustion. The boy rested his head on his knees, knowing he could not stay long; every minute would make it that much more difficult to continue. But there in the sheltered dark, Chris closed his eyes and wondered again how he could be so very far from home.

He had walked, it seemed, forever. Hope had faded. He no longer thought about the river's random turning and told himself that beyond he might come upon a tree, a stone, or feeding brook that had belonged to some part of his life . . . to those days of hunting with his father, and the wanderings that were his and Griper's secret.

A week now? No, it had to be more! That first night, when he had crawled from the river, was so far back in memory as to be nearly lost behind the jumble of other things.

And how much farther did he have to go?

Chris listened to the infinitesimal sound of falling snow, and sighed. It was time to do what he had come there to do.

He loosened the knots and pulled off his shoes. His feet were not frozen yet, but they were close to it. He remembered it happening once before, on a winter day when he had stayed out too long. Louisa Holm had sat him down before the fire and rubbed his feet with a rough towel until they tingled and glowed and he began to howl in protest.

The pine needles there were nearly dry and would, he thought, do just as well. Taking handfuls of them, Chris scrubbed his feet so vigorously that he was sure the skin was being worn away. But after a few minutes, circulation was restored. His feet, in fact, felt warmer than the rest of him.

Chris did not know whether he could prevent it from happening again; even the best of boots were not perfect in that respect. Still, he had an idea that might keep him going during the night.

He sprinkled a thick layer of needles into each shoe, and carefully slipped his feet back in. Then, before tying them again, the boy stuffed more needles into the spaces above his toes, around the sides, and finally at the heels.

It made them feel bulkier than ever, and he supposed the needles would shift around some as he walked. But even if the protection was spotty, it would be more than he had before.

Using the needles like that, and remembering how warm they had kept him before the weather turned bad, Chris hit on the notion of stuffing his shirt with them. It took several minutes, putting the needles in a handful at a time and distributing them front and back.

They scratched and tickled, and made him look like some half-completed spirit left over from the eve of Allhallows. Still, he knew the padding might make up for the coat he did not have, and only wished there was some way of tying his pants tightly at the legs so that they too could be filled with needles.

Tired, frightened, and with onrushing night adding darkness to darkness, Chris was tempted to stay where he was. He was sure he and Griper could curl up together in that nest and sleep with some small degree of comfort. But even then he felt the emptiness of hunger twisting and gnawing within, and there was a deep sense of urgency in that ghostly fall of snow that would not let him alone. Every flake, every silent swirling, added to the icy behemoth crouching across the miles.

They left the sheltering tree, went back into the dreaded and stinging snow, and found the river again. As if angels were dying there, the last of the light dimmed beyond the deepening veil, brightened for a hopeful but final moment, and was gone.

During the night there came precious intervals when the air beneath the clouds turned clear, and the space between river and forest glowed with a vague, spectral light. It was only the whiteness of the snow-covered ground, but Chris could not help grasping at those moments and searching the sky to see if it were not, instead, the first hints of morning.

There was not even a single, glittering star to signify the storm's passing, and as quickly as they had come, the intervals of respite were swept away again in a fresh deluge of darkening crystals.

In between, time was lost; he could not see Griper, and the world went elsewhere. In the deep emptiness left behind, only the sound of rushing water remained. The river, once a companion in dreams, once a thing of treachery and murderous intent, and for a while nothing more than a river, compass, and a source of food, was now that dreaming friend again.

Its voice came into his weariness and grasped him gently, whispering once more of those wonders waiting at river's end. Clusters of towns, bustling roads that went everywhere, so many people to talk to and know, and that great city . . . how marvelous it was even at night with bright lights shining against the dark! And it was not snowing there. Down in the lowlands, near the warming sea, winter brought only the quiet drumming of rain.

Yes, Chris thought. He saw those places now, saw them clearly, and felt the softness of their night pushing that other night away. Close to tears, he reached out for it and wished his father and mother could be there to share the joy with him. It was so very wonderful, so very . . .

The images dimmed and slipped into fog. They were gone, and Chris suddenly realized he was sitting in the snow, listening, while the silent flakes fell around him. Griper was there, too, waiting for him.

Startled, he stood up to slap and rub at his face until it stung. Whether he had fallen to his knees and actually slept for a while, or floated across the edges of delirium, he did not know. Either way, it was a frightening and dangerous thing, and could not be allowed to happen again if he was going to last out the night.

Chris took a deep breath and somehow summoned the strength to go on through the knee-deep snow. He was terribly cold, in spite of the needles stuffed in his shirt. His feet were an unending source of pain. But he welcomed these hardships, and concentrated on them, talking to Griper and shouting at the night as he counted his steps. He did not know how else he might avoid it, that drifting away from reality.

Chris went on and on, a hundred steps and then a hundred more. He could only wonder at the hour, and question the night. Grudging, cloud-ridden light was so far in the past, it had to be rounding the horizons and coming again to crack this shell that held him blind. And yet, if he were to abandon all memory and depend merely on what could be perceived and felt, then surely this night had slipped that cycle where the sun and stars moved!

And where, in all of it, was home? To walk so far and for so many days, and still not come to that familiar clearing . . . it was as if he, somehow, had been following a different river and not the one he had known all his life.

The idea grabbed at Chris and held. On the raft and in the dark . . . who could say he had not been swept past a final point of land where *two* rivers joined? For a moment the possibility faded when he remembered how he and Griper had met on the same side, but where was the certainty that that had not been by chance? Bent on finding his young master, Griper would not have hesitated to plunge in from land's end and swim to one side or another.

Chris considered the river he had been following, wondering if it had not been wider and deeper . . . and in his fright was not sure. And he thought about that night of walking in freezing rain, realizing they could easily have come to the rivers' joining without knowing. Yes, and in rain where older scents were washed away, who could say that Griper had not been as lost and blind as he was? Clouds had obscured the sun ever since. . . .

Chris stopped short, and stood in the silence close to screaming. But the thought that each step he took might be leading him farther from home was so appalling, so immeasurably grim, that he had to push it away. Such a thing simply could not be.

"Walk," he told himself. "Just *walk*."

In deeper cold and deeper snow, and in a farther part of the night, Chris wandered with the river and no longer looked or hoped for an end to any of it.

It was momentum, not strength, that kept him going. Habit, and not a conscious will to survive, kept him on his feet. But these things, though they held him upright far beyond reasonable expectation, were neither perfect nor immune to the forces gathered against them.

He fell frequently now, pitching headlong into the snow, and each time it was a little harder to get up. There was no warning, no way to avoid it; his mind was fogged by exhaustion and knew only the pain of motion, and he could do no more than stagger on until it happened again.

It was not until he suddenly stepped off into nothing, fell, and found himself not in snow but under water that the bright spark of awareness returned.

In an instant Chris was on his feet and thrusting himself into the air. Strangling on the water he had swallowed, he reached out blindly for the solid reassurance of the bank, *and could not find it!*

He knew then the full terror of that black place of tugging water and falling snow; he was imprisoned by both, and in the seeming suffocation of it the boy gave in to the wild electricity of panic.

Crying out, Chris thrashed through the water this way and that in a desperate attempt to escape, and only the loud shock of Griper's big voice was enough finally to make him stop.

Although he was up to his chin and gasping for breath, he realized that the water no longer moved. He was in no immediate danger. Obviously he had blundered into quiet shallows, into the outer edge of them where the first hints of a current could be felt. It was only a matter of luck, he knew, that panic had not taken him into the river itself. But all he had to do now was find his way out.

Chris decided against trying to return to the place where he fell in. It was probably still closer than any other part of the shore, but he did not want to go back to where the water moved. And besides, remembering how he had not been able to find the bank when he first stood up, Chris suspected he had been walking along a gradually narrowing finger of land that extended between river and shallows. It was something he had encountered several times, coming upriver; indeed, the same sort of thing helped form the shallows near home. But, in any case, it would be all too easy to wind up on the wrong side in the dark and go wandering into the river.

He wished Griper would stay in one place. The dog had stopped barking and was running back and forth. Chris could still hear his anxious whimpering, and occasionally what seemed to be rustling reeds and splashing feet. But the sounds were only vague and confusing, and he could not tell when Griper was closest to him. The river was too loud.

The *river* . . . yes, he told himself. Put it at your back and just start moving. It might not be the shortest way, but maybe it would be the quickest.

Knowing there might be deep, unexpected holes where he could suddenly be in over his head, Chris held his breath and made himself walk slowly across the sandy bottom.

The water lowered steadily, and after no more than a minute he stumbled into a thick bed of reeds. It confirmed what he thought he heard before, and it was a good sign. The bank might be fairly close; even if he kept going straight, he supposed he would soon find himself on swampy ground . . . yes, where he had heard Griper's splashing feet. But before he could decide on the direction to take, the reeds tangled around and threatened to trip him. He had to stop.

"Griper . . . where are you, boy?"

A big splash sounded somewhere to the left, and Chris stayed put, realizing that Griper was coming to him. The Labrador half-swam and half-lunged through the water until he reached his side.

Chris grabbed a fold of the dog's skin, and held on somehow as Griper pulled him back and along the edge of the reeds. Almost before he knew it, the water had retreated nearly to his knees. The dog jumped an instant later and was gone, and Chris stumbled forward to reach the bank.

His groping hands found the root of a tree, and as he felt it, looking for a grip, Chris suddenly found himself wondering. The narrow finger of land, the bed of reeds, and this root that was oddly familiar . . . they reminded him so much of the shallows near home.

The boy pulled himself from the water, and was afraid to hope. If he could only see! If only the clouds would part and give him starlight for one quick glimpse.

But he did not have a chance to find hope, or even give it cautious thought. The shock that struck him then was beyond belief. Coming out of the warmer water and standing for a few seconds in the open, he had given the freezing air time to burn through his wet clothes. It nearly paralyzed him from the waist down, and even now it was beginning to eat through the needles in his shirt. He had to move and keep on moving, somehow.

Chris took two frightened steps, and fell. He managed to get up, and walked perhaps a dozen yards before he cried out and fell again. But there was no getting up after that. Griper came to stand over him, and seeming to understand what had happened, only turned and walked away.

The boy simply no longer possessed the strength or the will to go on. He knew what it meant to quit now, but the driving and desperate little spark that had sustained him was gone and . . . and it did not seem to matter much. Indeed, after a few minutes, he felt sleepy and almost warm.

Chapter Sixteen

Christian Holm had come, in a darkness below the night, to a place of strange and dying dreams. They were like the last dim flickerings of a fire, and the end of a storm when clouds, glowing briefly within and muttering, have finally imprisoned the fretful lightning.

In the quiet that followed, there was a moment when words came to him out of nowhere; meaningless, echoing, they carried with their sounding the inexplicable smell of kerosene. But when the words had stopped, the snow beneath him fell away and Chris protested what seemed to be unwanted and unavoidable flight. It was a feeling of being swept upward, a helpless leaf in the wind, to flutter across the earth when he only wanted to rest.

Still, when flight was over, he did find a soft and gentler place. Paradise? He did not know. It was warm, and filled with sounds that were familiar but beyond understanding. For a while, he even knew the taste of food and sensed, beyond reluctant lids, perplexing lights and shadows. He tried to open his eyes, to understand, but hunger was gone, and gone with it were those nameless fears left over from a journey that once, in a moment of stirring, Chris thought he remembered. Paradise or elsewhere, it had to wait. The boy slipped from shallow sleep and found for a while a deeper, unknowing peace.

Not until much later did he awaken and discover that he had indeed come to paradise; an earthly one, yes, but to Chris paradise enough. It had windows, with the snow-bright sunshine of afternoon shining through, a cheery hearth and a drowsing dog and, above him, the faces of Eric and Louisa Holm.

". . . and that's about all," Chris told them. "Snow was coming down hard and I fell in the shallows. I remember worrying about them. The place seemed familiar. But it was too dark, and when I climbed out the air was so cold that . . . that's when I fell and couldn't get up again. Griper went on, and I thought . . ."

"He had abandoned you?" Eric shook his head. "Only long enough to come here and wake us."

"I guess he's pretty smart," Chris said, thinking about it.

"That big hunk?" Eric smiled and wearily sat down on the edge of the bed. "Well, maybe so. There sure wasn't any doubt about what he wanted me to do. Wouldn't even come in while I got my clothes. He waited on the porch, howling and barking until I came with the lantern and followed him." He paused and then almost whispered, "I didn't know what to think."

"But you knew it was me," the boy said.

"It had to be. You both disappeared the same afternoon, and after a couple of days we were certain Griper was with you and not just off on one of his little trips. When he finally showed up and made all that fuss, I knew you were out there somewhere. But I had no way of knowing how far, or what I was going to find. And when I saw you lying in the snow, so still . . ."

Eric Holm got up rather hastily and looked out the window. In the uncomfortable silence that filled the room, Chris had a chance to take a breath and become fully aware of what his disappearance had done to his parents. During the couple of hours that he had been awake, of course, there had been intervals when Louisa wept and Eric, as now, became too unsettled to speak; something of that near tragedy still clung to them. But those moments had dissolved with a word or a glance, to become smiles and bubble into the wet-eyed laughter of a family that is whole again. Then, there had been so much that needed saying and so many questions yet to be asked.

Now he saw how worn and thin his father was from long days of combing the forest and mountain slopes. With gloomy apprehension, his searching twice turned to the river and he had followed it some eight or ten miles even though it was unlikely that a body would be carried that far. The possibility of anything like a raft being involved had not occurred to him. Eric had returned in the dark of each hopeless evening to wait for dawn, to endure the nightmare of knowing merely that his son was *somewhere* in that wilderness . . . lost, hurt or dead.

Chris felt something shrink inside, and he turned to look at his mother who sat in a chair beside the bed. She had helped as much as she could, wandering in her distress to search and call beyond the clearing. But, mostly, hers had been perhaps the greater ordeal of waiting. With each passing and anguished hour the wilderness, which to Louisa had always been something of a rival and an adversary, seemed more and more to be finally winning. The days and nights, endless, had reached to the very roots of her being to leave her shaken, hollow-eyed and pale.

"I'm . . . I'm sorry," Chris said, and stared at the quilt covering his legs. "I guess it was pretty dumb, making the raft and everything."

His father stirred from his reverie and said, unexpectedly, "No. No, I'm glad you did."

"Eric!" Louisa was horrified. "What a thing to say!"

167

The tall Norwegian smiled, and life came back into the room. But he went to her, just the same, obviously regretting his choice of words. "I didn't mean it that way."

"The whole time, you were as sure as I was that Chris . . . and now you say a terrible thing like that!" She was caught between anger and tears. "Look at him! So thin and tired."

"I'm all right, Mom," Chris told her. "Really I am. And I won't do it again."

"Listen to me," Eric said quietly. "What Chris did was very foolish. He should've told us about the raft. If he had, I'd have fixed it so that it couldn't go anywhere. He didn't, though, and it's my fault. Always yelling at him for daydreaming." Eric stopped and did not look at either of them.

"Well . . ." Louisa dabbed at her eyes and could not find anything to say.

"Don't you see? Just his *wanting* to build a raft. That's what I'm glad about. He's growing up, and things like that are part of it."

Louisa looked over at the stove where a kettle of soup was still steaming. "He's only a child," she reminded her husband.

"Before all this happened, maybe," Eric said, and Chris saw something strange in his face. "But not anymore. Don't you realize what he did? He kept himself alive across a hundred miles of—"

"A *hundred* miles!" Chris interrupted. "I walked *that* far?"

"I don't know for sure. But the falls you saw

168

must be the same I heard a man describe at Bodwin's a few years ago. He thought it was about a hundred. The old boy was a prospector and knew this country pretty well. Considering how long you rode the raft, maybe he was close to being right. After all, that's no creek out there. She's big and she rolls right along."

Chris was awed by the thought. "It seemed like a thousand to me. But . . . it's still hard to believe!"

"Well, with a survey maybe it'd be only seventy or eighty. Who knows? Doesn't change anything, though. I don't know how you stayed on the raft all that time. And the way you managed to get back was quite a thing." Eric looked at Louisa again and gently placed his hands on her shoulders. "I'm afraid you don't have a little boy anymore."

Steadier, now, and seeming more like her usual self, Louisa brushed his hands away and straightened up in her chair. "He was a little boy then, and by my way of counting he's still only thirteen. And he needs looking after! If you will move your big hulk aside, I'll get him some more soup."

Chris groaned at the thought; he had already eaten two large bowls of it, plus a few slices of bread and jelly. But there was no stopping her. She was already up and not very gently tucking the quilt tighter around his legs. When she turned and went to the stove, Eric sat down on the edge of the bed and, smiling, winked at him.

Day was over. Darkness had come again. The lamp in the room below had been turned out and, while his mother and father slept, only the flickering glow from the fire reached into the loft.

How odd it felt to be in his own bed again, waiting for sleep and listening to the night. It was almost as if the last nine days had never existed.

Nothing had changed. The burning logs popped gently; Griper whimpered softly and chased phantom bears. Settling into the colder hours, the cabin made quiet little noises until it too seemed to sleep. Behind and beyond all this, made distant by the roof's mantle of snow, was the eternal voice of the river.

It did not sing this night, and neither did it speak. The river merely whispered as it rolled past the clearing; the words were lost. And what was it, really, but water tumbling over sand and stone, and a place for fish and frogs to live? What did it do except feed the searching roots of a million trees, and soothe the thirst of all that came to crouch at its edge?

Chris sank deeper into the quilts and closed his eyes with a sigh.

But somewhere far away, he thought, it *did* reach the sea.